DEADLY RELATIONS,
A MING DYNASTY MYSTERY

DEADLY RELATIONS

A Ming Dynasty Mystery

P.A. DE VOE

Drum
Tower
Press

Printed in the United States of America

Publisher's Note: This is a work of fiction. Names, characters, places, and incidents either are the product of the author's imagination or are used fictitiously, and any resemblance to actual persons, living or dead, business establishments, events, or locales is entirely coincidental.

Cover design by P.A. De Voe

Published by: Drum Tower Press, LLC

165 Bon Chateau Drive

Saint Louis, Missouri 63141-6081

http://padevoe.com/?page_id=177

ISBN: 978-1-942667-09-4 (paperback)

ISBN: 978-1-942667-10-0 (e-book)

To discover more stories about Ancient China, visit padevoe.com

I want to express my appreciation for Linda Harris Dobkins (AKA Jo Allison) and Sarah Thomasson, who read an early version of the story. Their insightful suggestions were helpful in plugging holes. As always, my writing is a collective task involving my invaluable editor, Renee De Voe Mertz, and my sharp-eyed husband, Ron Mertz. The image of bamboo with my name is by Sheow Chang. Thank you all.

CONTENTS

CHAPTER 1

Hong Shu-chang leaned back against the wall and watched as the examination runner piled his precious papers on top of the other unseen candidates' written responses. It had been a long week. He wondered how the time could seem to go so slowly and yet pass so quickly. He pushed his shoulders down, then pulled them up and held them for a short time, feeling the relief. Hours of writing caused a stiffness to settle onto his shoulders and spread through his back. He rubbed his hand across his eyes and sighed. He'd passed the district level examination with the highest honors, but that included only the district level candidates. The first rung to ultimate success, with two more rungs to go, each more difficult than the last.

For this second examination at the provincial level, he'd studied hard. He put in long hours day after day, memorizing the Confucian canons and their many commentaries, as well as developing a clear, analytic-style of thought and presentation of his ideas, which included calligraphy. For even this last was critical to winning a top placement. His style of writing showed the strength of his character and his thinking. Therefore, in spite of not being able to study under the best teachers, he felt confident. If he passed this second level examination he would bring glory to his father, his family, and his small village. He would be the first to have passed at the provincial level in the history of his family's ancestral home.

As he waited for the signal releasing him and the other candidates, allowing them to abandon their cells at the end of this grueling week, he stood and stretched broadly. Slowly, he started gathering up his brushes, ink, and inkstone; placing his leftover food in the wicker basket; and folding the blanket that had kept him warm in the chilly nights as he slept on the bench in his cubicle. None of the examinees had been allowed to leave while they wrote their answers. They slept on the the cell benches at night. Throughout the week, they were not allowed to speak to anyone for any reason. No extra paper could be brought in during the exam, either.

When he arrived one week ago, he had brought everything he thought he needed to survive this week-long testing marathon. What he didn't have with him, he'd have to go without. The Emperor was strict on that point. Thus, the government was vigilant against any possibility of cheating. Only the very best, the top five percent, would be given a pass and only they would be allowed to go on to take the third test, which was at the national level. Of the hundreds, even thousands of candidates, only the top one percent would be given a pass on that third, and final, examination.

But, for those who passed the third level, the bounty of the country would be poured on them: position, status, privilege, and wealth. Their and their family's future was guaranteed. It was Shu-chang's ambition to serve the Emperor as a magistrate, his civil and legal representative, and the prime intermediary between him and his people.

Shu-chang's goal held another, more immediate and personal desire: He had to pass the national examination at the highest level possible and get a top government position in order to bring status and a secure financial future to his family and his clan.

He breathed in deeply, held it, and then slowly allowed his breath to escape. He could taste and see his future. He would wear the black hat with its telling wings along with the badge of office emblazoned on his robe's chest. He would no longer be a poor, young man from a no-name village. Everyone would honor him and step out of his way as he passed down the street. His father would no longer have to toil in the fields. He would be proud of his son.

Shu-chang placed his hands on the blanket folded neatly in his lap and rested his head against the hard wall behind him. A slight smile tugged at his lips. The many, many sleepless nights he'd spent working and studying were finally beginning to pay off.

Suddenly, a commotion in the room aroused him. He straightened up and waited. Within a short time, a stern-faced fellow wearing a long, grey robe came to his cubicle. "You may leave now," he said, with a slight bow.

"Do you know when the scores will be posted?" Shu-chang asked.

"When they're ready," he answered curtly, thereby terminating any further conversation.

Shu-chang watched him slip along to the adjacent cubical and to the next candidate before gathering his writing implements, basket, and blanket in his arms. As he joined the lines of examinees exiting the building, he looked around at their faces. Most reflected the same exhaustion he felt; some looked hyper-confident, even arrogant; some showed anxiety, clearly concerned about how well they did; a few showed fear, perhaps already convinced they had failed.

None of these reactions surprised him. However, in studying the others more closely, he was surprised at the number of men who were significantly older than his own twenty-one years. Quite a few had to be at least in their thirties, and some even in their forties. In observing these older men, Shu-chang began to lose confidence. How many times had they taken the exam and failed? Undoubtedly, they came expecting to pass, but didn't. No matter how well a person knew the classics and could apply them, if he didn't surpass the level of his fellow examinees, he failed. Five percent. A man could be brilliant, erudite, have a good hand, and still be over-shadowed by others taking the exam.

He again scrutinized the faces of the others filing out of the exam rooms. Could he tell who knew more than he did, who expressed himself better, and wrote with a clearer hand than he did? Would he be coming back to these same rooms time after time to retake the examinations? As these thoughts turned over in his mind, and he moved in unison with other candidates, his confidence began to erode.

When he had arrived at the provincial capital two weeks ago, he'd met and befriended a couple of other candidates staying in the same inexpensive inn. They had gone around together to the different shops and carts buying the needed paper, brushes, ink, food, and bedding. Each looked for the best they could purchase with their meager resources. They had cast long looks at those who blithely purchased the finest of everything without a nod to the price. At the same time, each knew he was luckier than others to even be there.

Now Shu-chang was looking forward to spending the next several days with his new friends as they waited for the postings which would determine their futures. Being with them would help alleviate the excruciating tension of waiting. He silently gave thanks for their camaraderie. He started looking around for his new-found friends. Spying one just outside the gates, he picked up his pace to catch up with him.

Cutting in and out among those filing out in the same direction, he finally burst through the doors and reached the gates to the street. Once in the street, he stopped to peer over the crowd. Instead of finding his friend, however, his glance lit on a ruddy-cheeked, earnest-faced, young man wearing a short jacket and leggings tied just below the knee. It was Jin-fang from his village. He stood hopping from foot to foot on the edge of the street while perusing the crowd of candidates.

Smiling broadly, Shu-chang pushed through the crowd. "Jin-fang! How good to see you here," he called out through the noise.

A mixture of relief and concern crossed Jin-fang's face. "Shu-chang," he said. The strongly-built lad gazed critically at him. "You look like you could use a good stretching and training exercise."

Shu-chang laughed. While he and Jin-fang were the same age, his friend was much more muscular. From an early age, he had been interested in martial arts and had picked up quite a bit here and there over the years. As Shu-chang's friend, he insisted he also practice every new-found technique. Thus, while not nearly as proficient as Jin-fang, Shu-chang had benefited from their practicing together. He stretched. "Yes, several days sitting in one small cubicle does make me feel stiff."

He expected Jin-fang to make a joke about this, but he didn't.

"Shu-chang...," Jin-fang said. His voice wavered. He paused.

Was there bad news from the village? Shu-chang wondered, watching his friend's face grow red and his eyes flicker toward the ground.

"Shu-chang," he began again. This time there was no denying the sorrow in his voice. "I..." He stopped and looked

5

at the throng milling around them. "Let's go to a wine shop for a bite to eat."

Shu-chang clapped him on the shoulder. "Indeed. I am so glad to see you here today. What a grueling experience. But well worth it, if I pass," he grinned. Jin-fang had always been one of his biggest supporters, so he expected him to say something positive like: "Of course, you will bring honor on our village." Or some such thing. But Jin-fang said nothing; his eyes slid to the right and left, as if avoiding something. An uncomfortable feeling spread up the back of Shu-chang's head. Something was amiss.

They went to the nearest wine shop to order a plate of simple rice cakes. Recently freed candidates filled the room, noisily drinking and eating. Shu-chang found an empty table at the back of the room. Clearly, Jin-fang wanted to tell him something important. The din provided a privacy screen for their conversation.

Shu-chang ordered before turning to his good friend. "So, what brings you all the way to the capital," he opened.

Jin-fang unhappily tugged at the sleeve on his short jacket. "I have bad news," he began quietly, then stopped.

Shu-chang leaned in so he could hear better through the engulfing clamor. "Tell me what's happened."

The young man looked up, his eyes sorrowful. "There's been a terrible tragedy at home. Four days ago, a group of bandits came into the village. Your father, uncle, and the other men on the defense team went out to stop them." His rhythm sped up, so that Shu-chang had to lean closer to hear his soft, quick telling of the happenings. "Our defense team fought bravely against the bandits' knives and rice sickles. The thugs injured several of the security detail. And killed two of them."

He stopped again and pulled at his tunic as if searching for a way to tell the rest of the tale. Finally, his face red, he blurted out: "The two men killed were your father and uncle." With tears in his eyes, he looked up. "I'm so sorry."

Shu-chang sat in shock, not believing what he'd heard. This couldn't be right. He must have misunderstood. Surely, Jin-fang meant his father and uncle were wounded. A tragedy, yes, but Shu-chang would go home and take care of them. His mother had died many years ago living the hard life of a dirt-poor farmer's wife; he was used to taking care of his father. His uncle had not yet married. He always said he'd marry as soon as he could afford a wife and family—someday, but not yet. Unfortunately, that day had never come, and now, if what Jin-fang said was true, it never would. No family of his own. No son to care for him in his afterlife.

Shu-chang waited for Jin-fang to correct the mistake he'd made in telling his story.

Jin-fang sat as if he'd exhausted his ability to speak; he remained mute.

Finally, Shu-chang said, "So *fu-chin* and uncle are injured. Who's taking care of them now? Did they have to go to the temple for their injuries?"

Jin-fang lifted his head and, with tears shining in his eyes, said, "Shu-chang, your father and uncle are dead. In the battle, they were both badly wounded and lost a lot of blood. The villagers carried them immediately to the temple, but they died soon after. You must come home to bury them."

Dizziness overcame Shu-chang. He pressed his fingers to his eyes. "I don't..."

"I've come to help you. I've been waiting for the examinations to be over. Your father would have wanted that. He never would have wanted you to leave before you had a chance to finish them. But now we have to go home," Jin-fang said.

"Yes, yes, of course." Shu-chang no longer heard the noises around them. His life had stopped. He was dimly aware of his friend's continuing commentary, but he understood nothing. He couldn't think, his mind a stunned blank.

Since his mother's death, his father and he were a unit. His father believed in him unconditionally; he was his main supporter in every way. His father did everything to make sure there was money for Shu-chang's education.

Sure, the village was proud of him and hoped that he would bring them glory, and perhaps even a modicum of wealth, but they had nothing to offer for his livelihood. It was all any of the families could do to survive themselves. Frequently, families quietly sold off their daughters because they could not feed another mouth without everyone else suffering. His father had put everything into Shu-chang's education, never complaining about the fact that he had to work twice as hard out in the fields to buy ink and paper as Shu-chang sat inside studying. His father believed his son was brilliant—at least brilliant enough to pass the third exam and achieve a position of power and status. As Shu-chang had heard many, many times, such a feat would bring more than wealth, it would bring glory to their whole ancestral line. It was his father's dream, and his.

"Did you hear me?" Jin-fang asked.

"Yes. We'll leave in the morning." He'd find out about how well he did on the examination later, somehow. Perhaps he could arrange for one of his new-found friends to let him know if he'd passed. There was no possibility of remaining in the provincial capital until the notices came out. It would be shameful for him to stay in any case.

Jin-fang began to get up to leave, but Shu-chang put a hand out. "Stay. We'll eat and then go."

"I'm not hungry."

Shu-chang kept a hand on his arm. "Eat. You've been waiting for so long."

Jin-fang cast a quick glance which reflected an uneasy gratitude. "If you insist. I could eat something."

The two sat in silence, munching on the rice cakes and drinking hot water. Finally, Shu-chang asked, "Has the magistrate found the criminals guilty yet?"

Jin-fang looked down at the old wooden table, gouge lines crisscrossing its surface. He mumbled, "When I left they hadn't been caught. No one knows who they are."

"What! How could people not know who did this? If there was a fight, lots of people must have seen them?"

"Maybe, but no one will come forward and say who it was."

"You're telling me that no one will identify the killers?" He looked at his friend. " Can you tell me who they are?"

"No. I was out in my field at the time. I didn't see anything. I think it was a gang that has been harassing our village for some time. You remember last year when our village was pillaged? I think it's the same gang, but I don't know. And no one who was in town is saying anything."

"Do you think they're afraid?" Shu-chang asked, yet certain that they were.

"Um-hum. People are terrified that if only one or a few are caught, the rest will come back and take revenge on whoever identifies them."

Shu-chang closed his hand into a tight fist. "They must be caught. What is the magistrate doing?"

"He sent his soldiers out to look for the bandits, but they've disappeared. No one seems to know where they've gone."

Shu-chang's knuckles turned white as his fists closed even tighter. "I'll find them. They'll not escape so easily."

Jin-fang nodded. "You can look during the three-year mourning period for your father, when you have to be at home."

Shu-chang stared at his friend, as if just now processing another important part of this event. "Right. A time to grieve and to discover who did this." A husky tone of pain and anger crept into his voice.

Jin-fang again looked up at his friend. "You'll have to work your father's fields. There's no one else and you need the livelihood." A look of concern crossed his face. "How will you be able to study? The next exam will be even more difficult than this one. And how will you ever be able to buy the paper, ink, and candles you'll need, much less pay a teacher?"

Shu-chang nodded. He didn't want to seem callous and unfilial, yet, unbidden, these thoughts had raced through his mind as well. His father had given up everything for him, and now he had to do it himself. But how? Could a farmer also be a scholar? Could he work in the fields all day, cook his own food, clean his own clothing and room, and still study the long hours necessary to succeed?

He stared at Jin-fang. "Father had faith in me; he sacrificed his whole life for me, for my success. I cannot betray his expectations." He dropped his head into his hand.

After a moment, he sat up. "At the same time, I must not let their murderers go free. They must be held accountable," he said, anger filling his voice. "My duties are many, but I must do as much as I can. I cannot let my father and my clan down."

CHAPTER 2

The trip back home was solemn, their conversation filled with funeral plans. Shu-chang had to buy coffins for his father and uncle and order Buddhist prayers to be recited and give gifts to the officiating monks. He needed to purchase spirit money, incense, food, and all of the other things the deceased would require in the afterlife, which was exactly what they would require in their worldly life. And, of course, he had to have proper mourning clothing for himself. He mentally began tallying up the cost of all these things. He didn't know how he could possibly pay for it, but there was no choice. These were his responsibilities now. At the same time, he had to find out what needed to be done in the fields. He asked Jin-fang if anyone fed his father's three chickens.

Jin-fang laughed. "You don't have to worry about them. Although it's always good to give them scraps, they find plenty to eat in the yard. What you do need to do is collect their eggs. That's your food." He shook his head. "Your father didn't teach you much about farming, did he?"

Shu-chang smiled balefully. "No. He always said my job was to study; he'd take care of the rest."

The grin faded from Jin-fang's face; they continued on in silence. Eventually, they saw a cluster of simple houses made of beaten-earth and covered with thatch roofs in the distance. Shu-chang paused, gazing at the quiet scene. A handful of peasant homes. What kind of person would think anything in there would be worth killing for? Composing himself, he nodded to Jin-fang, and they continued on.

As they entered the village, several of his neighbors came up to express their sympathies. By the time they'd arrived at Shu-chang's home, he was worn out.

A low mumble of voices came from inside. He pushed the door open and a wave of onion and garlic greeted him. His stomach growled, reminding him that they hadn't had a meal since they'd left the provincial capital the day before.

"Nephew! You're just in time to eat," a robust man in his middle years called out to them.

"Uncle Xin," Shu-chang said, spying his mother's brother. "How good to see you."

"Now is the time for family to pull together," Uncle Xin said. "With your father and his brother gone, you have no family left. Your mother would have wanted me to be here for you."

It was all the young man could do to keep from crying, as much from relief as from gratitude. Uncle Xin was right, Shu-chang had no family left on his paternal side. He hadn't seen his maternal uncle since he was a child at his mother's funeral, yet here he was, ready to help.

Two of the villagers rose from three-legged wooden stools and went to squat down near the wall. "Sit. Sit," Uncle Xin said, pulling the stools close for Shu-chang and his friend.

As they sat, his uncle's wife, Aunt Nu-er, brought over a plate of rice cakes topped with sliced green onions. Both young men devoured the cakes before saying any more.

"I hope you don't mind, but I've gone ahead and started

preparing for your father and his brother's funerary needs," his uncle said. "And your aunt made mourning clothing for you."

As he finished speaking, Shu-chang's aunt brought out a bundle and unfolded the rough woven hemp-colored cloth, which, out of filial duty and respect for his father, Shu-chang was to wear for the next three years.

At the sight of the mourning clothing, He fell on his knees, doing a full kowtow toward his aunt and uncle to show his respect and gratitude. In this the darkest moment of his life, they had come to support him.

The next few days passed in a haze of activity. Fellow villagers came and went, bringing food, offering condolences. Shu-chang tried to find out more about how his father and uncle died; who was suspected and where they might be, but no one could—or would—tell him anything in detail. It was as Jin-fang said: The murderers seemed to have disappeared. Even the local security team claimed to have no knowledge of the murderers they'd fought with. The whole situation confounded and depressed Shu-chang. He didn't believe the culprits were unknown. Yet there was nothing he could do until after the funeral.

On the day his father and uncle were buried, a small band playing gongs, cymbals, and a drum, along with a contingent of Buddhist monks, led the burial procession of Shu-chang, his mother's family, and his fellow villagers, as they accompanied the bodies to the cemetery. He was sure his father would be pleased with the turn-out and with the enthusiastic cacophony of loud, clanging music played on the way out of the village. The brassy, syncopated sounds were certain to frighten away errant spirits and ghosts. He was indebted to his maternal uncle for such a fine funeral. While no one spoke of it, Shu-chang was keenly aware that such a display would have put him deeply into debt.

That evening, once most people finally left—after sharing a generous dinner prepared by Aunt Nu-er and a few of the village women—Shu-chang sat outside in front of the house with his friend Jin-fang, his uncle, and a few neighbors. The topic had switched to the weather and the possibilities for the year's rice crop. The general consensus was that this year was not going to be any better than the last several years' harvests.

As they sat quietly talking, a sturdy fellow strode up to the house.

"Is Hong Shu-chang here?" His loud voice drowned out all other chatter.

"I'm right here," Shu-chang said, rising up from his stool. As he moved toward the newcomer, he noticed some of the village men shrank back into the house's shadow.

The stranger pulled an envelope out of his sleeve and handed it to Shu-chang. "This is for you from Master Gao."

"What is it?" Shu-chang asked as he took the envelope and turned it over, examining the seal.

"I deliver the messages; I don't read them," the fellow said with a smirk. After raking over the villagers with a quick cursory glance, he turned on his heel and strode off into the darkness.

Shu-chang opened the envelop and held the note up. The filtered moonlight caught the paper, but the moon's glow wasn't enough to allow him to read it. He went into his house where the women were clustered around a light and tried again. His uncle followed him and stood near the doorway.

Shu-chang read the letter. Perplexed, he glanced at his uncle, then re-read it. His throat closed. This couldn't be.

"Is it bad news?" Uncle Xin asked.

Shu-chang stared at the paper in his now trembling hand. A frown settled on his face, and he passed the note to his uncle. Only the sound of crinkled rice paper could be heard.

The women sat still, watching. A few of the men had silently come into the small room to see what had happened. The room had become stifling, the air almost too thick to breathe.

"Your father turned the title of his land over to Master Gao in order to have him shelter his land against taxes," Uncle Xin said flatly, after a brief look at the note.

A low mumble spread through the room like a thick coating of sorghum. Shu-chang looked around. The villagers were all muttering as they nodded their heads in understanding. Most of them had done the same thing.

When Master Gao was a young man he'd passed the third and highest examination in the country. That feat gave him—and more importantly, his family—many special privileges, including exemption from land taxes. As a result, many families in the surrounding villages decided to deed their land over to him as a shelter against Imperial taxes. In return, each family paid Master Gao a fee for the privilege of his protective umbrella. The fee was smaller than what they would otherwise owe in taxes. Importantly, the agreement came with the undocumented understanding that each family would continue to work their land, which they still owned by custom. Over the years, this system had worked to everyone's advantage. Until now.

No one had seen Master Gao in over a year. In the meantime, his grandson, Gao San-fu was now in charge of the family business. The word among the villagers was that Master Gao was no longer personally involved. Some even quietly gossiped that his mental capacities had diminished, although no one dared say this out loud. Under San-fu the land fees had gone up considerably. Many were now paying even more than the government taxes would have been. But it was too late to change the documents. Between the bad crops over the past several years and the increased fees demanded by San-fu, the villager's livelihood was severely threatened. More and more of them had trouble feeding their families. A few had already been forced to sell their daughters to decrease the number of mouths to feed.

Given this dilemma for the majority of villagers, Shu-chang looked luckier than most. He was only one person and had a productive parcel of land. The work would be hard, but what peasants' life wasn't hard?

"Don't worry, Shu-chang. Your father and uncle worked this land for their whole life even though the title is in Master Gao's name. It doesn't matter. You'll also work the land," one of his fellow villagers said.

Uncle Xin shook his head. "No. This letter is demanding that Shu-chang leave. It says the agreement was with his father, not with him. Master Gao wants the land."

At that, a roar broke out as everyone, men and women, spoke at once. This declaration was new. No one had ever been turned away, thrown off their land. This threatened not only Shu-chang and his family's farm, his inheritance, but everyone. A sense of unease washed through the room.

"What else does the letter say? What is to become of the land?" demanded a gaunt man rising from his position on the floor.

Uncle Xin again looked down at the letter. "It says that a fellow named Gao Tan will come within a couple of days to take over the house and land."

Again, the villagers all began speaking at once, discussing, arguing. Shu-chang sat in shocked silence. He had just lost his father and uncle to a murderer and now he was about to lose his ancestral land, too. What had he done in his former life to deserve such a terrible fate?

Eventually, his neighbors wore themselves out in useless arguing, coming to no conclusion. They were powerless. They could complain. They could rage against their fate, but they could do nothing, and they knew it. Shu-chang began to realize that a few of them started looking at him as if he'd contracted a disease and, if they stayed, his bad fortune would spread to them. At first two men slinked away, then others followed, offering Shu-chang a feeble good-bye before slipping out the door.

After everyone had gone, even Jin-fang, Shu-chang sat alone with his aunt and uncle.

"What will you do now? Do you have any plans, any place to go?" Uncle Xin asked.

Shu-chang shook his head, staring at his hands folded in his lap. "No. This has all happened so quickly. In a matter of days I've become an unfilial son. A son who, although unintentionally, has failed his own honorable father. A father who had done everything to help him succeed. I can neither continue my studies and pass the third exam nor farm my ancestral fields."

"You don't have any friends you could go to at this time? A teacher you had? Someone in the capital?"

"Sir," Shu-chang spread his hands around, as if encompassing the room, "this has been my world up until today. I studied at that table while my father toiled in the fields. That was our life. My teachers were few and were themselves itinerant scholars who had to scrape together a living however they could."

Aunt Nu-er spoke up. "Husband, Shu-chang has studied hard and taken the second examination. He is a scholar with some talent. Could you find a position for him in your clan's school? They've been without a teacher for many months now. And even then, the last teacher lacked ability."

Uncle Xin brightened. "Indeed, that is a good idea." He turned to his sister's son and said, "Shu-chang, your aunt is right. Our clan school has ten students and no teacher. Would you be willing to come to your mother's home town and teach? As far as I know, none of our young men have shown much flare for scholarship. However, I'm sure that if you'd come, they might have a chance to succeed. One or two might even be able to pass the examinations. There is little pay; however, you can live with your aunt and me. Such a position would also give you a chance to continue your own studies."

Shu-chang glanced back and forth between his aunt and his maternal uncle. He felt a flood of relief and gratitude. His paternal family was gone; he was the only one left. What a fragile link between the world of the living and the dead! The success of the family line now rested on him. He had to succeed, no matter what.

He nodded. He would willingly and happily work in his uncle's clan school. He glanced quickly around the room once more. Although he wouldn't admit it out loud to anyone, not even his uncle, he would be glad to leave this simple, one-room house and turn his back on the life of subsistence farming. This opportunity was a golden shaft of light in a dark room.

"I deeply appreciate your offer of both the school position and living in your home."

"Good. I'm glad. I have always wanted to do more for you since my sister died so young and couldn't be the mother you needed."

"No," Shu-chang shook his head, "even in death, my mother is with me, as I am sure my father is, too. They guide my thoughts."

Aunt Nu-er agreed. "Our home isn't far from here. You can tend to their graves without trouble. You will have time to show proper respect for your father."

"There is one other thing I should tell you, since you've never been to our town," Uncle Xin said. "Most of the people living there come from two clans. The Xin clan and the Gao clan. The Xin clan is not big. As I said, our school only has ten students. The Gao clan is much larger and they own most of the land. Whereas our clan temple is modest ..."

"Small," Aunt Nu-er injected.

"...modest in size, their temple is imposing," he finished, giving his wife a slight scowl.

Shu-chang stared at his uncle. "Is that the same Gao family the villagers were talking about? Does Master Gao live in your town?"

Uncle Xin pursed his lips and nodded. "The same. Our town is the region's market town and, therefore, significantly larger than your village. You will find that there are many amenities there—more shops, restaurants, temples, and general street entertainments and activities than you have here." He nodded again and pushed his hair behind his ear. "While it's not a city, it offers a lot more than you've been accustomed to in your father's village."

Shu-chang did not miss the note of pride in his uncle's voice. Clearly, even though the Xin clan was the minority in the town, Uncle Xin was proud of his ancestral home.

"We have men who share your love of learning and the classics. I can't say for sure, but you may even find a mentor for your further studies."

At his uncle's last words, Shu-chang shifted on his stool, his brows knit together. "I haven't even learned whether I've passed the second examination. It may be days or weeks before I know."

"I've no doubt that you have—and with the highest honors, I'm sure," Uncle Xin said.

"May the gods hear you and push my work forward." Shu-chang grinned, but then he twisted his lips into a grimace, exhaled, and said, "So far my fate has not been good. And when I looked around after the examination, I couldn't help but notice how many very bright young men were there taking the exam at the same time. My fate may not be as I wish. Perhaps I have to work out some past bad karma before I can move forward."

"Even if that is so, you're not alone. We're here to help you. Don't despair," Aunt Nu-er said.

Shu-chang looked with gratitude at his aunt and uncle. They offered him not only a place to work, but a chance to repay his father both by finding his murderer and by succeeding in the examinations.

CHAPTER 3

Although tired from the long walk, as Shu-chang approached the market town, he held himself straighter and picked up his pace. He wanted his new neighbors to see a strong, determined teacher, not a youth exhausted in both body and spirit. He had found closing up his house and turning it over to Gao Tan to be more difficult than he had anticipated. After all, even though he'd always hoped to eventually live in a much grander house as he took on important and prestigious positions, that simple place had always been his home.

He adjusted the small parcel he carried, pushed his morose thoughts to the back of his mind, and strode into the town.

The first thing he noticed was how much busier it was than his village. Businesses and street carts lined the main street, selling not only all manner of food, clothing, trinkets, and religious paraphernalia, but also a wide range of services, including writing documents or letters for illiterate clients, repairs for every tool a kitchen or farm needed, and haircuts. This town was close to his home, but it was a world away. His father came here to sell his excess crop and to purchase whatever they needed, but Shu-chang had remained at home, studying, preparing for his future—for their future. Now this was his future.

As he slowed down, moving through the street and observing the ebb and flow of activity around him, he caught sight of a strange young woman coming towards him. He noted how deftly she negotiated the crowds despite the bulging parcel tucked beneath her arm. Equally striking was her expression, for although he found her features themselves to be rather plain, the set of her face suggested an almost masculine self-possession and sense of authority. Her clothing, too, was mannish: a long, brown, roughly woven outer robe hid her figure while a singularly odd, broad-brimmed hat stuck out over her shoulders. Its brim shadowed her face, protecting it against the sun. As she grew near, he glanced down and confirmed that, indeed, she did not have the bound feet of a woman from an elite family. Perhaps she was of the merchant class, he thought. And yet that too seemed strange, for now even in merchant families conscientious parents—those especially concerned about the social status of their daughter's future marriage—would have bound her feet. Lotus feet were becoming a passport to a good marriage, since they indicated a woman of duty and beauty. Her resulting inability to walk without assistance also signified the wealth of her husband's family. It meant that they had servants and did not need to rely on their women to perform menial household tasks.

Shu-chang was intrigued. He may have been raised in a poor household, but even he knew what a good woman should look and act like. And it was nothing like this figure approaching him through the crowd. What did such a woman do?

The stranger passed by without a glance in his direction.

She seemed to be totally focused on something else. As she passed, a small bag dropped out of her parcel. She continued on, not realizing what had happened.

Shu-chang quickly retrieved the bag before it was smashed into the dirt. He felt it: one side was soft and fragrant, but the other seemed to hold something quite hard. The scent was not particularly pleasant. He sniffed it. Not perfume, he noted and smiled. No, not perfume for such an aberration as this young lady.

"Miss! Miss!" he called out after her.

The woman stopped and turned slightly towards him, inquiry written on her brow.

"You've dropped this." He yelled over the street noise, dangling the bag so she could see it.

She inspected the parcel she was carrying and stuck a finger into a hole at the bottom. Vexed, she stared at the bag he held out to her.

"Oh, it fell out! Thank you for finding it." Her fingers pinched the hole closed as she firmly trapped the parcel between her body and her arm. She stepped lightly and graciously toward him to retrieve the smaller sack.

"I tried to pick it up right away, but I'm not sure everything inside survived the fall." As he handed the item over to her, he smiled into lively, inquisitive, dark eyes.

She took the bag, opened it, and examined the contents. She partially pulled out a short, rounded bottle, ran a finger over it and stuffed it back into the bag. "Everything looks fine. Again, I can't thank you enough."

With that, she closed the pouch and put it on top of her parcel, which she now cradled in her arms. She nodded at him once more and continued rapidly down the street, leaving Shu-chang standing alone, staring after her and bemused. He watched her until she disappeared through a large door, which was protected by brightly painted, ferocious door gods standing on each side of the entrance.

He shook his head. This town was certainly different from his home village and even the city where he'd recently taken the exams. There, women knew their place and showed proper deference to the men around them—at least publicly. Well, usually. He thought of the few experiences he'd had where this hadn't been the case. He scratched at his hair line, thinking. Entertainers. Yes, she was probably an actress. They did behave differently.

He grinned. He may like this town. There were so many strange and curious differences from what he had known so far. With that thought playing though his mind, he proceeded to his uncle's home.

Uncle Xin had arranged for all of the students to convene the next morning in the clan temple. As a small clan with only a few students, the cost of building a separate school was considered a waste of money. Classes were held in one of the temple's side rooms. Although somewhat snug, it had proven more than adequate over the years.

As Uncle Xin solemnly introduced him to his class, Shu-chang observed each student. His main thought: *what a rag-tag bunch*. They seemed to be only slightly more cultivated than street urchins. Not one appeared to be capable of true scholarship. He sighed. Was this his future? Teaching students who didn't care, as long as they could read a ledger and work their numbers, so that they could run a business?

As his uncle talked on, Shu-chang continued to peer out at them, but his thoughts turned inward. He no longer listened to the admonishments telling the young men to study, work hard, and do well. Instead, he recommitted himself to make the best use of this time to find his father and uncle's murderers and to study himself. His throat caught as he wondered how he did on the examination.

He needed not only to pass, but pass at a high level in order to come to the attention of potentially influential men. Men who could assist him in his struggle to achieve success and bring respect to his father and his ancestors. Waiting, not knowing the results, weighed heavily on him. His initial confidence had long since dissipated. He now felt fate had turned against him.

Eventually, after one more stern order to study hard, his uncle left Shu-chang with his contingent of students. As their new teacher, he stood before them, doing his best to appear austere and demanding, with his arms folded, hands tucked into his sleeves.

"We'll begin with each of you reciting the Confucian Classics. Begin with where you left off with your last teacher."

No one spoke. All eyes turned down, as if each boy found something of great interest on top of the marred table in front of him.

"All right. Beginning with you," he thrust a finger at the boy sitting close to him on the right. "Start reciting."

The boy looked up to Shu-chang's chest and muttered, "Sir, I don't remember my lessons."

Shu-chang caught his breadth. "You don't remember? What was the last lesson your teacher gave you?"

"We didn't get very far," the boy said, head down.

"Hum. How about you?" Shu-chang pointed to the boy next to him.

"I'm sorry, Sir. I don't remember, either." He straightened in his chair. "But I can read and write all that is important."

Shu-chang was surprised at how cheeky the boy was. He'd expected them to show more respect to their teacher. Was this the way people acted in this town?

"What is your name?" Shu-chang said.

"I'm called Xiao-ren."

The other students snickered.

Shu-chang looked the young man over. Xiao-ren meant Little Man. Although Shu-chang guessed him to be about sixteen years old, he was already considerably taller and more muscular than his fellow classmates. Xiao-ren wasn't the name his parents gave him, it was merely what people called him. Shu-chang neither smiled nor chastised him for being out-of-line. He merely nodded.

He went down the line. Although no one else acted as out-spoken as Xiao-ren, only a couple of his new students could recite even a small passage from the Confucian Classics. Apparently, they had only intermittently had a teacher, and then only for a very short time. Even though the boys were old enough to have learned at least half of the Classics, not one of them had. They had learned how to write and to do math from an elder in the community, but that was all.

His duties were going to be tougher than he'd thought. No matter. He thought of Uncle Xin and his father. This was his only chance; he must do all that he could.

"We'll start the Classics at the beginning. All together." He opened the book and began to read. After a while he stopped. "Now read the passage together in unison."

A few of the boys followed directions.

"Stop. Stop. I said in unison. I want to hear everyone reading," Shu-chang demanded.

The boys began again. This time everyone seemed to be reading. Shu-chang watched them intently to be sure they were following his orders.

When they finished, he rapped the table. "Now I want you all to memorize this passage by tomorrow's class. You can begin now until class is over. Each of you will recite it without errors, do you understand?"

The class nodded, eyes again on the table.

Tomorrow he would find out what kind of students he truly had. Maybe this wouldn't be as terrible as it first appeared.

As the boys recited the passage aloud in order to memorize it, Shu-chang noticed that Xiao-ren sat holding his head, moving his lips, but not actually saying anything. He stepped in front of the young man. Xiao-ren didn't notice him, because his eyes were not on the book; they were closed.

Shu-chang picked up a small rod and forcefully struck the table in front of Xiao-ren. The crash brought all to attention. Xiao-ren almost fell off his stool; the others snickered.

"Silence!" Shu-chang roared. An immediate and tense silence filled the room.

"What do you think you're doing?" Shu-chang demanded of Xiao-ren.

"Resting. I'm tired."

His response seemed to bring another level of tension into the room, as the others wondered how Shu-chang would react to such brazenness.

"You will rest when you're at home. Not now. Not here. Now you will memorize your lessons." Shu-chang's tone and demeanor left nothing to the imagination. He picked the rod up again and let it rest in both hands as he spoke.

Xiao-ren, scowled but nodded. As the class resumed their recitations, he joined in.

After the class ended and Shu-chang joined his uncle for tea, he asked about Xiao-ren.

Uncle Xin inspected his face for a moment before answering. "I suppose he gave you some trouble," he began. "Every teacher we were fortunate to have left because of him. He's a terror."

Shu-chang waited. He didn't want his uncle to think he had failed on his first day, nevertheless, a sense of dismay began to settle over him.

"He's your mother's second cousin's only son. So unlike his sister Xiang-hua. She is dutiful whereas he is rebellious. She is studious whereas he is well...." He waved a hand in circles in the air, sighed, then went on: "His father struggles every day to control him. I don't know how it happened, but he seems bent on disrupting and destroying everything Chu tries to teach him." He grimaced. "Even the clan elders have had no luck. He's been beaten until he bled, but it was no good."

"He seemed unusually sleepy for such a terror," Shu-chang noted.

Xin nodded. "He had started working for the Gao clan, mostly nights. It brings in some money. Not that the family needs him to do it." He emptied his tea cup and placed it back onto the table. "He will be your most difficult challenge."

Shu-chang refilled his uncle's cup while unhappily thinking that all he needed was another challenge.

CHAPTER 4

Xiang-hua strode up to a massive wooden door bookended by two brightly painted divine guardians who protected the family within from evil. The Gao family was the wealthiest in the town and their entrance reflected their status. She knocked on a smaller door embedded in the larger one's right side. It opened immediately and she stepped over the threshold and into a courtyard lined with verandas on three sides.

The lean, middle-aged servant allowing her entrance greeted her. "Good morning, Sister."

"It is a good morning," she agreed. While unrelated, the servant called her Sister out of respect for her position. "How is Erh-xi-fu today?"

The man's fingers worried a long hair growing out of a mole on his chin, his face pinched. "Not well. My wife tells me that Erh-xi-fu has been ill for several days now. That is why Mistress called for you; she doesn't seem to be getting any better."

Xiang-hua nodded and followed him across the bare courtyard, a cloud of dust rising around their feet. His wife was Erh-xi-fu's maid, so he knew the secrets of the women's inner quarters, even though he never entered that closed-off area or talked to any of the other women of the house.

At another small door opening onto the courtyard's veranda, the servant stopped and knocked. A solemn, elderly maid opened the door to the rooms of the Mistress, the matriarch of the house. Without a word, she stepped back to let Xiang-hua enter. Then, just as quietly, she closed the door behind her and led Xiang-hua inside.

A late-middle-aged woman leaned against pillows on a wooden *kang* set along the far wall. Although beginning to show signs of age, she remained a beauty. The peach colored, softly glowing silk tunic she wore showed off her delicate complexion. Large, elaborate turquoise and silver hair pins held her glossy black hair up and away from her face. Next to her on the raised platform, a stubby-legged, dark wood table held small plates of fruit, two blue and white porcelain cups, and a tea pot on a rimmed wooden platter. A tea kettle sat off to one side of the wooden tray.

"Madam," Xiang-hua bowed in greeting.

"Sister, I'm glad you were able to come so quickly. Come and sit here with me," she said, indicating a place across the wooden tray from her.

Xiang-hua smoothly slipped onto the kang and tucked her legs under her.

"How is your Grandmother, Yi-po? No one has seen her in a few days. I hear she's not well."

How quickly gossip travels, Xiang-hua thought. "She's in good health. One of the Emperor's concubines was not well and she specifically requested for Yi-po to come and serve her. She had to leave for Nanjing immediately and will be gone for some time. We don't know how long. Whatever the Emperor decides."

The Mistress immediately sat forward. "How wonderful!

The Emperor. Her medical knowledge is indeed great. I always knew she and her family were exceptional," the woman gushed.

"You are too kind." Even though she fully agreed with the assessment, politeness demanded a show of modesty. Xiang-hua's grandmother had been trained from her childhood on by her own mother and father; she came from a long line of highly respected, knowledgeable physicians. In keeping with tradition, no one outside the family could be privy to their medical secrets. As a result, the women of the family were highly desirable as wives for families who wanted their sons to become physicians or who were also physician families and wanted to gain another branch of medical technique or knowledge. Such was the case with her grandmother. Her grandfather had also come from a famous medical family.

"What is it I can do for you, Madam?" Xiang-hua asked.

The woman glanced at the doorway. "It is Erh-xi-fu. I'm afraid she is ill. Again."

"Tell me her symptoms," Xiang-hua said, dropping her eyes so that she could concentrate on every word.

"This is a family problem." Her hand automatically dropped to her stomach, which she absently patted. "And, it's more than just this one time. Erh-xi-fu came into our home as San-fu's second wife almost a year ago and she still hasn't conceived." She looked intently at Xiang-hua. "His first wife never gave him a child and now this."

She couldn't accuse her daughter-in-law of being barren out loud. It would be too unlucky. "You must cure her." She drew her long silk sleeve over her mouth. "You can do it. Your grandmother and grandfather taught you many things. You have helped other women in town to conceive. You must help my daughter-in-law."

Xiang-hua bowed her head in understanding. "I'll do all I can. First, tell me her symptoms."

The woman's lips drew tightly together as she thought about the her son's second wife. "She can't keep anything down. She was thin when she came and now she's gaunt. She's weak and can do very little. She's almost no help around here." A note of complaint snuck into her voice.

"Well, you can see for yourself. My maid will take you to her. She's resting in her room."

Xiang-hua rose and followed the maid through the women's quarters to a door off to one side. They entered without knocking to announce their arrival.

A form lay on a rumpled kang. A pale, delicately featured face was turned toward them. The patient's eyes were closed, and she seemed unaware of the noises they made as they entered. The only other person in the room was a child who sat on a stool next to the woman. Xiang-hua guessed her to be about nine years old. She immediately stood at attention as they entered.

The maid, who had accompanied Xiang-hua, ignored the child and stepped over to the kang. She gently said: "Erh-xi-fu, the doctor is here to see you."

The young woman slowly opened her eyes and rose up on one elbow. "Sister, thank you for coming. My mother-in-law told me you were called." She coughed and slumped back down onto her bed.

Xiang-hua nodded to the maid, excusing her. As she left the room, Xiang-hua went to the kang and pulled up the stool the child had vacated. Sitting, she took the young woman's arm. The sleeve fell back, exposing bruises on her pale skin. Xiang-hua turned the hand up and held her wrist. She held it for some time, eyes half closed, concentrating on her fingers recording the pulse. Standing once more, she placed the hand on the the woman's body. Continuing her examination, she pressed on her abdomen, then, loosening the robe's top, she felt her neck. It was then that she noticed the red welt circling her neck. Finishing her examination, she resumed her seat on the stool.

Xiang-hua chose her words carefully. She began with Erh-xi-fu's monthly menstrual periods. "Your periods are light," she said, basing her observation on the woman's pulse.

"Yes, I have not missed a one, but they have become quite light."

"You have had normal relations with your husband since your marriage?"

Erh-xi-fu blushed and a look of anxiety crossed her fair face. She clutched the robe holding it close to her neck. "Yes."

Xiang-hua rested a hand on the young woman's upper chest. "Tell me about your neck."

Erh-xi-fu nervously looked around the room.

"No one is here except your little charge. The maid's left," Xiang-hua assured her.

"It's nothing."

Xiang-hua kept her hand reassuredly resting on the woman's shoulder and remained silent. Waiting.

Erh-xi-fu looked up at her with pain in her eyes.

"I was unfilial." She stopped, then with a deep sigh, began again. "I tried to commit suicide. To hang myself. But my mother-in-law found me before I could succeed."

Xiang-hua patted her chest. "It is not unusual to not get pregnant so soon after marriage. Sometimes it takes more than a year, or even longer. You don't need to be ashamed."

Erh-xi-fu shook her head. "It's not that," she blurted out. "I don't want a child. I want to die."

Now Xiang-hua began to understand, she had seen this desperation before in other newly married—and sometimes long-time married—women. Their home life became so onerous that they saw death as the only reasonable alternative. Xiang-hua's grandmother often counseled her that what these women needed was someone to talk to in order to release their tension and stress. And, along with dispensing medicine, listening was one way she as their doctor could most help them grapple with their fate.

"Tell me about it," Xiang-hua said.

Tears began to trickle down her cheeks, but she quickly brushed them away. "San-fu is not happy with a sick wife." She looked away. "And he is impatient about not having a son."

"It makes him angry," Xiang-hua said. A statement, not a question.

"Yes."

"Can you go to your mother-in-law? She could intervene for you. You mustn't misjudge her."

"I'm not misjudging her," Erh-xi-fu said, her tone carrying a surprising note of resentment. "She is almost as bad as her son."

Xiang-hua thought of the bruises on her arm and nodded.

As if taking her nod for affirmation, Erh-xi-fu went on. "Because I am so ill and not of much use around the house, my mother-in-law is often very irritated with me. If I can't do something, she becomes angry and beats me."

"And San-fu?"

"At first San-fu was good to me: kind, thoughtful, even forgiving of all my wifely faults. But this last month he has been very, very tense. He comes home angry. Nothing I do pleases him. Beating me seems to release his tension. It's like he has to hit me to feel better. It's not about producing a son —that's his mother's view. He even complains to her about everything. She blames me for his bad temper." She paused and pulled the end of her sleeve down, covering her bruises.

"You can give me your medicines. The family can pay a lot of money to 'fix' me so that they will have a son. None of that will change my fate and what will happen."

"Look at me," Xiang-hua said. The young women reluctantly turned toward the doctor. "Right now, everything seems impossible except death, but change is always possible. Trust the future. I will help you in whatever way I can. Do you believe me?"

Erh-xi-fu slowly nodded, but then glanced away.

Xiang-hua knew she only had a short time to help her before she gave up once more.

"All right then," she said and took up her parcel. "I'll let your mother-in-law know about the medicines you'll need to increase your *qi*. It's much too low. In the meantime, I want you to rest. I'll inform your mother-in-law that for a short time you are not to be disturbed—not even by your husband."

Erh-xi-fu's hand released its grip on her robe. Nevertheless, the question of whether this young doctor could actually help her never fully left her eyes.

Xiang-hua again gently patted the other young woman's shoulder, as she had seen her own grandmother do so many times when treating patients. Staring down at Erh-xi-fu's prone figure, she hoped that she could be as good a physician as her grandmother was.

Before leaving the house, Xiang-hua went back into the mother-in-law's room.

"Mistress, your daughter-in-law's *qi* must be built up in order for her to produce the sons you want. Tomorrow I'll bring medicines for her. In the meantime, Er-xi-fu must eat better than she's been eating. Give her plenty of dark meat and soup. No uncooked vegetables. As much rice as she wants."

"Are you saying you believe she can still produce a son?" the woman asked with both hope and skepticism.

"We must build her up first," Xiang-hua replied cautiously.

Once out of the compound, Xiang-hua looked around at

the normalcy of small clusters of people passing by and at the market stalls. Breathing in the dust and dirt of the streets, she felt cleansed after being in the Gao house.

"So, you are consorting with the high and mighty, eh," a raspy voice called out to her.

Xiang-hua smiled at hearing the familiar voice. "Good morning, Granny," she said, using an honorific in greeting the figure closing in on her.

The term immediately identified the elder as a midwife and as an intimate of the women who were her clients. In her case, she also aided the women behind closed-doors by running errands for them, such as shopping. She moved freely in and out among the wealthy families. She also knew most of the merchants in town since she shopped among them quite frequently.

A sprightly woman of indeterminate age stepped up to Xiang-hua, who surmised that she was as old as her own grandmother. And just as feisty.

"Undoubtedly you were in to see Erh-xi-fu," she said knowingly.

Xiang-hua laughed. "You know what's happening in this town before it happens," she said, hoping she wouldn't reveal too much about Erh-xi-fu's affairs through this conversation. It wouldn't help her relationships with her patients if Granny learned intimate details about them because of her own care-less talk. Whatever the elder woman knew could become town gossip or be used as a surgeon's knife for extracting favors or saving families and relationships. This seemingly harmless elderly woman was quite the entrepreneur. Although, as far as Xiang-hua knew, while Granny used her skills and information-gathering ability to her advantage, she had never intentionally hurt anyone.

"It's my business to know everybody's business," she cack-led, then added more soberly, "That girl has gone through a lot." She squinted up at Xiang-hua. "It's possible that together we can help her."

"You are too kind, Granny. I can only offer my poor skills to the family. I am not good enough to work with such a respected treasure as yourself." Xiang-hua bowed slightly while frantically thinking of how she could extricate herself before Granny trapped her into one of her schemes.

At that moment, the bell tower rang the time.

"Oh, listen. I'm late getting back home. Please forgive me. Now that my grandmother is not home, I have much to do."

"Go on your way, Xiang-hua. We'll talk another time."

With relief, the young doctor turned and sped down the town streets, away from Granny and her too frequently disastrous plots.

CHAPTER 5

Exhausted, Shu-chang fairly collapsed on the chair behind his desk. He'd just released his students for the day. All in all, he thought, the day hadn't been as terrible as it could have been—as he'd feared it would be.

Some of the boys actually memorized the passage he'd assigned yesterday, and everyone had memorized at least a few lines. He'd have to be even more strict with them. How would they have a chance at a better life for themselves and their families if they didn't learn more?

The image of his student's simple faces passed through his mind. He grimaced. No matter what, they would learn under his tenure as teacher. He owed his uncle that.

He rubbed a hand over his eyes. His debts of filial piety and of honor to his family—his father, uncle, and now his mother's brother, Uncle Xin—seemed to be growing and with little results except the bare minimum. While grateful to have work, he was also dismayed. Was this what his future will be? Survival at the lowest level? And, if so, how was he to pay his filial debt to his family?

He shook his head. He couldn't let such morose thoughts

take over; they would interfere with his successfully carrying out his duties. Turning his attention away from these concerns, he collected his few things and walked back to his uncle's home.

As he entered the house and approached his uncle's sitting room, he heard voices.

"Come in, Shu-chang," his uncle greeted him warmly. "This is Master Xin Chu, your mother's father's oldest brother's son." The complicated kinship relationship told Shu-chang exactly what he needed to know: that this was his first cousin one generation higher than him, on his mother's side of the family. Being such a relative and older than him built an automatic bond between him and Xin Chu. A bond of interdependence.

After sharing greetings and general observations on the town, Chu said, "I understand from your uncle here that you are an excellent teacher and one with a broad mind."

"I am a mediocre teacher, but I try," he replied modestly. Clearly, with his cousin's reference to "his broad mind" the older man had something to ask him, something that might offend him, or that was at least somewhat objectionable.

He began to feel uneasy. He was in a delicate position. Whatever the request was, it would be hard to impossible to say no. He glanced quickly at Uncle Xin, but he appeared relaxed as he poured tea for them.

Chu coughed. "I have a daughter. She is young and of moderate intelligence," he began. "Nevertheless, from the time she was a child she liked to read, which we encouraged. She has learned a great deal under the guidance of her grandparents, but she—we—would also like her to increase her knowledge in the classics." He toyed with the tea cup in his hand. Finally, he looked up and said, "Would you be willing to teach her? Perhaps one day a week, after classes? Or maybe even two days a week? Whatever you feel you can?"

Shu-chang was surprised at the request. It wasn't that he was against educating girls. They had to learn reading, writing, and numbers in order to properly run a household. But not many girls, he was sure, were capable of truly understanding the subtleties of philosophical thinking. Women were pragmatic beings, not given to deep thinking. They could learn to read the classic on Filial Piety—on how to behave toward one's parents-in-law—but, really, the Confucian Classics? He didn't believe this was reasonable to expect.

Yet, how could he say this to his cousin? It would embarrass everyone, including Uncle Xin, who'd clearly thought this was a legitimate plan.

"Of course, I'd be happy to teach your daughter one day a week for an hour or two after classes," he said. One to two hours a week wouldn't take too much of his time away from his own studies and his search for his father's and his father's brother's murderers.

"Excellent!" Chu clapped his hands together and rose. "I'll have my daughter brought over right now. She happens to be visiting your Aunt Nu-er at this moment."

Before Shu-chang could change his mind, he heard a slight commotion outside the room. A young woman, who appeared to be about seventeen years old, entered the room. She wore a multi-hued embroidered, green robe tied at the waist with a long red sash. Shu-chang immediately noticed that she walked with a strong gait and not the mincing glide of most women of her class. He looked at her feet. They were unbound. Then he looked at her face. Although dressed in finery and with her hair done up and held in place with a silver comb, this was undeniably the young woman he had met in the streets when he'd first arrived.

"This is my daughter, Xiang-hua," Chu announced.

She bowed, eyes politely lowered.

"Pleased to meet you again, Xiang-hua."

Chu and Uncle Xin looked at them in confusion.

She raised her eyes and smiled. "Yes, in town. You found my herbs and bottle." She turned toward her father. "I dropped a packet out of a hole in my medicine bag and he retrieved it for me."

"So, fate has already brought you two together," Uncle Xin said.

"Master Hong Shu-chang has agreed to teach you once a week after his day classes," her father said. With a stern face but kindly eyes, he added, "Be sure not to shame your family by failing."

Xiang-hua bobbed her head in both acknowledgment of the admonition and acquiescence.

"You will find her to be an exceptional student," Uncle Xin said. He could brag about her since he was not her father. "She has already learned much and has developed a reputation as a poet in the area. However," he smiled, "she is most known for her medical skills. She has apprenticed under her grandmother since she could talk and shows some talent in the medical field. Most of the homes in town call on her grandmother and her for their women's problems."

"You mustn't boast about her poor abilities," her father inserted. "She will become too proud."

But Uncle Xin just smiled and proffered a plate of dried fruit to his guests.

Shu-chang tried to observe his new student without showing too much interest. Nevertheless, he was now even more intrigued by this young woman than when he'd first seen her bustling along on the street.

It was as if she were a new kind of being. He'd known young farm women who didn't have bound feet and who could go about the village carrying out their duties, but they were uneducated and not at all refined in their speech or overall demeanor. They were raised to be hard-working

41

farmer's wives, nothing more. They weren't expected to be able to read or know even the most basic numbers because that would give them more education than most of their husbands. And everyone knew it was never a good thing to have a wife know more than her husband. Such a relationship would prove inauspicious for the entire household.

On the other hand, elite families wanted their daughters to be able to read, write, and keep the household ledger. They ran large households with staff and complicated social relationships while their husbands handled the affairs of the outside world. Everyone he'd ever met or seen from this class wore lotus shoes over their tiny feet. Such feet emphasized their femininity and, at the same time, their ability to conform to and obey the wishes of their superiors.

He quickly glanced down at Xiang-hua's ample feet peeking out from under her skirt. What did such feet tell about her? His eyes slid over to the side to observe her father. What did such feet say about her father and his family?

"Shu-chang, are you listening?" He heard his uncle ask. Jerking his head up, he focused on the lock of hair falling over his uncle's forehead.

"Yes Sir. What was that, again?" Shu-chang asked.

"I asked if you wanted her to recite anything in particular right now or perhaps create a poem? To give you an idea about her education so far." His uncle said and grinned at his apparent discomfort, while choosing not to mention its obviousness.

A knock on the door saved Shu-chang from having to answer. A tall, lean man wearing a short jacket and pants that met his socks at the knee burst into the room almost before Uncle Xin had finished saying "Enter." His sinewy arms and legs, along with his clothing, indicated that he was a laborer. "Sir, there's been a fire in the warehouse district on Min Road."

"What?" "Turtle's egg!" "How did this happen?" Uncle Xin and Chu exploded simultaneously. Xiang-hua, eyes wide-open in shock, took a step forward. Shu-chang stared at the messenger, then at his uncle. A warehouse fire meant a great loss for the town. Not to mention that the fire could easily jump to the other wooden businesses and houses in the area.

"Call out all the men in our neighborhood to put out the fire. We will need every available hand," Uncle Xin said.

The man spun on his heel and dashed back out of the room.

"Xiang-hua, you come along. Bring your medicine bag," her father said.

She immediately rose and hurriedly left the room, returning only a moment later. Shu-chang realized her home had to be adjacent to Uncle Xin's in order for her to have come back so quickly.

The four headed out for the warehouse district.

CHAPTER 6

As they joined the surge of men speeding through the streets, they could see flames reaching above the surrounding buildings' rooftops. By the time they arrived, it was too late to save the block of warehouses. The fire had engulfed the entire area. Finally, they went to a wall of ferocious heat and halted. If they came any closer, the heat would blister their skin. They stepped away and back along with the rest of the crowd.

Shu-chang looked around. A man in a stiff, black hat and long, dark robe caught his attention. While the hat was informal, it clearly marked the wearer's position as a government official. The magistrate. His face was a mask of anger and frustration. He yelled at the men around him and at his soldiers, but nothing could be done. It was too late.

Shu-chang heard the magistrate ask if anyone had been caught inside. A bystander called out that there hadn't been any workers and that he thought he saw the watchman outside after the fire started. So, no. He didn't believe anyone was inside.

The magistrate yelled a few more orders, before spinning

around and marching back down the street with his guards. Shu-chang watched him leave. The villagers had told him about the magistrate. He'd come to this insignificant market town because he was required by law to personally investigate all murder cases under his jurisdiction. The deaths of Shu-chang's father and uncle. While in the area, he temporarily resided at the comfortable and grand Gao residence. Shu-chang watched him intently and wondered what he could have discovered about his father's and uncle's deaths when he stayed here in the comfort of Master Gao's compound. A day's walk from the village where they were murdered.

"It will burn itself out. It won't jump the road and burn other buildings. Nevertheless, the men will remain and keep an eye on it," Uncle Xin said. Turning toward Xiang-hua, he added, "I'm glad your services weren't needed."

She nodded, eyes glued on the fiery warehouse.

Still watching the magistrate's fading figure, Shu-chang said, "Now his resources will be split between cases, and this will likely take precedence for the next few days. At least until he determines whether the fire was accidental, or arson."

Uncle Xin and Chu nodded.

"Any evidence still out there will only grow colder." The corners of his mouth turned down. "This new disaster will give the murderers plenty of time to get away."

"The magistrate has already interviewed everyone he thought might have seen anything. He's also carried out an examination of the bodies and where they were found," Xiang-hua said, shifting her medicine bag from one arm to the other.

"Yes," Chu agreed. "According to local gossip, the murderers were gang members. If so, you will learn more about them right here than you will anywhere else. More than in your home village, certainly."

Shu-chang raised his eyebrows and again pressed his lips together.

"This is a market town," his uncle added. "All information flows through here. Nothing happens within its parameters without someone knowing. And a gang has been active in the area for many months. Some have suggested this is their headquarters."

"Or at least their boss's headquarters," Chu amended. "Don't despair. This magistrate isn't so bad. He'll find the killers."

Shu-chang stared at the fire; its smoke filled his lungs and stung his eyes. If this was the place to find his father's killer, he would do it. Nothing would distract him.

The next day Shu-chang's students couldn't settle down. He rapped the desk with his rod; he yelled at them for their poor performance and inability to study. Nothing helped. All they wanted to talk about was the fire and the finding of two bodies in the ashes. Flames had quickly engulfed the building, making the smoke and heat overpowering to anyone caught inside. Burned beyond recognition, the bodies were unidentifiable. A rumor claimed they were the arsonists, who hadn't made it out of the warehouse in time after they set the fire. Others insisted they were laborers or guards who worked there. One rumor asserted that the dead men were enemies of a powerful gang that infiltrated the town. It was impossible to tell.

At lunch, Shu-chang gave up and let his students go home after giving them a hefty bit of memorization. The assignment absolved his conscience; he convinced himself that he had fulfilled his duty as a teacher. Nonetheless, he had little confidence that any of them will have completed even half of their homework by the next day.

He stepped out onto the veranda and almost collided with Uncle Xin.

"Shu-chang, I must speak with Xiao-ren immediately."

Shu-chang grimaced. "I'm sorry, Uncle. He wasn't in class today."

"Where are your students?" Uncle Xin looked into the empty room.

"I gave them a lengthy assignment to study at home," Shu-chang replied. His explanation sounded feeble even to his ears. He only hoped his uncle wouldn't think he was already shirking his duties and fire him.

"Yes, yes. Too much going on. The whole town is in an uproar. They're blaming the fire on that new gang and are demanding the magistrate do something. He's already sent out several of his staff to investigate the site and to find every person who could be involved. Quite a number are waiting at the Gao compound right now. The magistrate set up a temporary court in the Gao courtyard and the interview process is underway."

Shu-chang studied his uncle's flat face, anxiety emanating from his worried eyes.

Uncle Xin then glared at the school room as if finding an enemy in its spare, uninhabited space. "A soldier came to take Xiao-ren to the court for questioning."

Shu-chang was stunned. "Xiao-ren. Whatever for? He's just a boy."

"He's been working for San-fu at the warehouse for many months now. Xiao-ren is sixteen and old enough to both work and get into trouble." He couldn't keep the irritation out of his voice. "He should have been here studying over those months. Just as he should have been today."

"It's only for questioning," Shu-chang said.

"Any contact with the court means trouble," his uncle replied, striking the doorjamb with the side of his fist.

There was no doubt about that. Even the innocent could end up destitute after paying off all of the people involved in the court process. And he cringed at the thought of the tales he'd heard of accused prisoners being tortured in order to get them to confess to the crime. Yet, Shu-chang had faith in the system. It was necessary for the magistrate to cover every conceivable avenue. Isn't that what he wanted from the magistrate in his father's case?

His uncle added, "Perhaps he's down in the warehouse district. Many are still there, hoping to be the first to hear what and who caused the fire. It's the biggest event of the year. A real draw for the boys. I'll go down and find him. It wouldn't be good for the court to think he's avoiding them." He frowned and shook his head. "That one is nothing but trouble."

"I'll go with you."

They walked through the streets still heavy with smoke, each holding his sleeve over his mouth to filter the air. The pollution kept most people in the shops, tea houses, and taverns. It wasn't until they came up to the burned skeleton of the warehouses that they saw clusters of men standing about. One particularly noisy group caught their attention. The men all seemed to be talking over one another, arms flailing in all directions as they made their points. Shu-chang thought he heard the name Xiao-ren as they got closer.

At the sight of Uncle Xin, the group briefly fell silent.

"Xin! Where's Chu's boy?" a short, hefty man called as they approached.

The others stared at Xin and waited.

"Studying. As he should be," Xin lied.

"Isn't that the new teacher there with you?" the man asked.

Shu-chang spoke up, "All of the students are working on an assignment."

The group smirked at that and several started talking at once again. The sturdily-built fellow was the loudest. "It's common knowledge that Xiao-ren was involved."

Xin blanched. "What are you talking about? He's just a boy."

Shu-chang looked away at that remark.

"He was unhappy with San-fu because the boss doesn't put up with a sloppy hired man—no matter what his age. Xiao-ren knew he was about to be fired and was angry," another in the group said.

"Who told you that?" Xin demanded, his face turning a dark red.

The man smirked. "Lots of folks. Those young people don't work like they should. Lazy, I'd say. Why pay them for a day's work if they don't do anything?"

The men around him nodded.

"I'd heard Xiao-ren had a fight with San-fu's foreman. When that boy was supposed to be guarding the warehouse, he stole. Rice went missing. He thought no one'd notice, but he got caught. Gao doesn't hire stupid foremen," a wiry young man said.

"Yeah, he's a thief," a couple of others added.

Xin exploded, "Chu is a good man! How dare you accuse his son of such things? What evidence do you have? Hearsay. Gossip. You're nothing but a pack of trouble-makers, liars, and discontents."

At that, most of the men looked away and stepped back, but the short fellow held his ground, glaring back at him.

"We'll see what the magistrate says," the wiry fellow said and spat on the ground.

If Xin's face could have gotten darker, it would have. He was about to retort, when he spied a small figure on the other side of the street. He grabbed Shu-chang's arm and said, "There's Granny. Xiang-hua said she's been nosing about. She's always full of useful information. Let's go talk to her and see what she's learned."

Xin scowled once more at the men around him before dragging Shu-chang across the street.

Granny saw them coming and gave them a small bow.

"This is not good," she said, eyes flitting across the street to the knot of gossiping men standing amidst the warehouses' remains. "Did they tell you Xiao-ren's been implicated and already many think he may even have started the fire himself?" she went on.

Xin nodded. The short walk across the street allowed him time to regain his composure and his face was now a blank slate. "I'd heard. Of course, it's nonsense."

Granny pursed her lips. She paused, as if holding back bad news.

"What? Now what?" Xin asked.

"You've heard those people talking," she said, "but they are only passing around what they've heard. They don't really know."

"Yes. Yes. That's what I said: it's nonsense," Xin said.

"But where there is smoke there's fire," she said cautiously.

"Or just a smoke screen for another perpetrator," he rejoined.

Granny grinned, but it wasn't a happy smile. Shu-chang thought it looked more like a grin of reluctant acceptance.

"I've just returned from Chu's house," she said.

"Chu's house? Why did you go there? Xiao-ren isn't home."

Granny ignored his comment. "The magistrate's soldiers were there looking for him. And, as you say, he wasn't there." She paused. "But they did find something," Granny went on.

Xin glowered at her. "Don't play with me, Granny. What did they find?"

"Bags of rice with the Gao family symbol, their mark, on the bags."

Xin didn't betray his emotions. "Are you sure? Did you see them or is this also hearsay?"

"I was there. I saw soldiers coming out of the house, carrying bags of rice. Each appeared to have the Gao mark on it."

"Right. Probably San-fu sold the rice to Chu or to Xiao-ren," Xin said in defense.

Shu-chang noticed, however, that his uncle's shoulders suddenly slumped and his voice lost its edge.

"It's possible," Granny said. Her words were noncommittal, but her tone suggested there might be a problem. "The court will decide."

Shu-chang looked at his uncle and thought about his earlier comment that any contact with the court was dangerous. Was the Xin clan about to experience the full impact of that involvement through Xiao-ren's transgressions?

CHAPTER 7

As Shu-chang sat with his uncle back at the house, Chu showed up. He looked worn and defeated; a complete transformation from the day before when he had come in with Xiang-hua. He collapsed into a chair, propped his elbow on its burnished wood arm, and covered his face with his hand. He slowly rubbed his face and emitted a low moan. After a couple of minutes, he raised his head to face Shu-chang and Uncle Xin.

"The town believes Xiao-ren is involved in setting the fire," Chu said.

They nodded.

"Now that they've found the remains of two bodies in the ashes, whoever set the fire will also be charged with murder," Chu continued.

"He's a difficult boy, but he wouldn't do such a thing," Uncle Xin said. his voice hard with anger.

Chu looked up, anguish written in his face. "You know that and I know that, but how are we going to prove his innocence? His running away makes him look even more guilty."

The three sat in silence for a while before Shu-chang felt

he could speak. "When we were at the warehouse this afternoon, we only heard about Xiao-ren. Any more news? Has anyone else's name come up? Anyone at all who could be involved?"

"No. Only our Xiao-ren. But, I ask you, how could, why would, such a young fellow burn down a building? I don't believe it's a spontaneous act. It required planning." He stuck out his chin. "Frankly, Xiao-ren has never shown any inclination for organizing anything. He doesn't plan; he simply reacts. That's his problem. He hasn't learned to keep his emotions under control. I don't believe he'd create a plan to revenge anything because he's so erratic," Chu said, his voice rising.

Shu-chang cringed. He understood Chu's explosion, his frustration and anxiety over his son's unpredictable behavior. But, if anyone heard Chu say this, it could certainly be considered even more damning. Nothing would disturb the magistrate more than an out-of-control, erratic, and emotionally angry young man. And, how much planning did it take to start a fire in a powder box such as the warehouse anyhow?

"The magistrate will discover the truth," Uncle Xin said.

"Not necessarily. He must find the culprit quickly. The people are demanding it. Xiao-ren is an easy answer." Desperation and despair he couldn't hide caused Chu's voice to waver.

Shu-chang spoke up: "Perhaps you could investigate yourself."

The two looked at him in surprise. Then, Uncle Xin brightened. "Of course. Even if the magistrate is led astray, you could prove his innocence and take the evidence before the court." He looked straight at Shu-chang when he said this.

Shu-chang licked his lips and shook his head. "I meant you, or others in the clan, could do it."

"We could help where needed, but you're an outsider with an important position, Teacher, and the town's people would talk to you more easily than with us," Uncle Xin said.

Chu looked at Shu-chang, hope springing into his eyes for the first time. "You would save Xiao-ren's life."

Shu-chang let out a long breath. How could he work on this while at the same time teaching all day and trying to find out more about his father's murder? He glanced at his uncle and Chu. Their faces reflected anxiety, fear, and a tinge of hope.

His uncle had offered him a lifeline with his teaching job and a free place to live. How could he deny his request? He felt caught between loyalty to his father and appreciation and loyalty to his mother's brother.

"But, of course, now that he'll be doing an investigation for us, we need to be clear about Xiao-ren and what we know so far," Uncle Xin said, assuming Shu-chang would, indeed, investigate. "Beginning, for example, with the fact that Xiao-ren had been working with Gao San-fu for about four to five months now."

"Shu-chang, you must already have seen that Xiao-ren is nothing like his sister, Xiang-hua. She's steady, hardworking, and reliable. He's always been restless, stubborn, and always wanting more. Really, I must admit, often quite unfilial. There've been many a time I needed to beat him to get him to behave," Chu said. He passed a hand over his eyes for a moment before continuing. "I think he went to work for San-fu to spite me. San-fu's grandfather passed the third and highest examination, giving him and his family special privileges and rights. Therefore, through his grandfather's power and influence, San-fu now controls much of the town and its affairs. Xiao-ren is captivated by his power."

"Did Old Master Gao's son also pass the examinations?" Shu-chang asked.

"San-fu's father? No. He was never much of a scholar. He failed the first level examination three times and gave up. He was better at the finer things in life," Uncle Xin said disparagingly.

"Like women and parties," Chu added. "Master Gao's grandson, San-fu was a bit better. He at least had a head for business. Although he followed his father in his taste for women and wine."

"As Chu said, much of San-fu's power comes from his Grandfather's position, not from his own work, nevertheless, he runs their family business and the lands under his grandfather's control with an iron, unyielding hand. He is brutal and will brook no interference." Uncle Xin said.

"Yet Xiao-ren went to work for such a man?" Shu-chang said, mystified.

"Because San-fu and his clan run the town. Our clan is a poor second. While we're all righteous people, we are insignificant farmers and tradesmen. We cannot compare with Master Gao and the Gao clan. As I said before, Xiao-ren was bewitched by San-fu's power and influence. He can do anything," Chu said frowning.

"I wonder why people have accused Xiao-ren of stealing from the Gao warehouse? There was a claim he was to be fired as a bad worker, so why the second accusation?" Shu-chang said. He wanted to add, *if the accusation wasn't true*, but he refrained.

Uncle Xin and Chu exchanged a look that told Shu-chang more was coming.

"In the past, maybe about a month ago...," Xin began.

"Two weeks ago," Chu corrected.

"Humm. Yes. Well, two weeks ago, San-fu's foreman came to the clan elders and complained that Xiao-ren had stolen rice from them. We weren't able to find any evidence and told them so. The foreman agreed to take Xiao-ren back as an employee, since we didn't find anything. Eventually, they found the bag of rice, which had been moved to another of the Gao warehouses."

"But the damage had been done," Chu said. "Even though Xiao-ren was found innocent and returned to work under the Gao foreman, rumors still went around that he'd stolen."

"It is difficult to turn off the rumor mill once it's started," Shu-chang said.

"Wisely put," Uncle Xin said. "So, you'll help us?"

Shu-chang didn't have any choice. "I will do everything I can."

CHAPTER 8

Three students were absent the following morning: Xiao-ren and two brothers. That reduced Shu-chang's class size to seven. At this rate, he wouldn't have any students remaining by next week.

"Where are Zhang-zong and Zhang-lung?" he asked.

Blank faces greeted his question. Finally, one brazen soul raised his hand. Shu-chang nodded at him.

"They're not coming anymore."

"Not coming? Why not?"

A couple of the boys snickered behind their hands. Shu-chang glared at them.

"Their father said schooling is too expensive and they're needed in the fields."

"This is their clan school. Their father isn't paying me, the clan is." Shu-chang said, exasperated by the low regard their father had for learning.

"But we have to have ink, an ink stone, a brush, and paper. That costs, too," the boy brazenly responded. A couple of the boys nodded in agreement. The others stared, wondering what their teacher would say.

He didn't reply, and instructed the students to begin reciting their memorization homework instead. Even though the boys still wanted to talk about Xiao-ren and the fire, Shu-chang managed to keep them on track until the end of the day, when he finally released them.

As his charges slipped quickly and thankfully into the late afternoon sunshine, Shu-chang set the room straight. Xiang-hua would be coming for her first lesson and he wanted to be ready for her.

He soon heard a melodious voice greet his aunt outside in the courtyard. A young woman appeared silhouetted in the doorway. She carried a parcel holding her writing implements and a package of rice paper. Her fine cotton skirt swished softly over the brick floor as she stepped into the room.

"Good afternoon, Teacher Hong," she said. Her voice was quiet, but he thought he heard a lilt in it. He hoped it meant she was glad to be here.

"Come in, Xiang-hua. You may sit there," he pointed to a nearby table and crude, three-legged stool.

"I saw your class leaving, " she said as she deposited her writing materials and began to lay them out on the table. "Poor Xiao-ren. This terrible warehouse situation is causing him a lot of trouble, even here, in school." She shook her head. "He's missing so much." But then as if looking for something positive to say, she added: At least the other Xin boys are able to study."

He grimaced at the thought of his students. "Well, your brother was not the only one absent today. The brothers Zhang-zong and Zhang-lung did not come. And they may remain absent." He didn't know why he added that last part. He certainly didn't want her to think he had failed when he'd just started.

Xiang-hua raised her eyebrows in an unspoken question.

"Apparently, their father thinks schooling is a waste for

them. He wants them to work the fields, not study." His frustration at what he thought was a narrow and unenlightened viewpoint came through his every word.

Xiang-hua nodded. "Yes. Their father is a simple man. It's not that he wants to hold them back; it's just that he doesn't see any other future for them. Perhaps you should go speak to him. Let him know how important this opportunity is for his sons."

Shu-chang frowned. "The boys also said their father didn't want to buy their writing materials, claiming they were too expensive."

Xiang-hua nodded. "His farm, like most farms in the district, has not done well these past couple of years. Many families are living on the edge."

"So, there is no use in talking to their father."

"Well, if you don't want to try...," she left her thought unfinished.

He threw an irritated glance at her. It wasn't his fault their father's farm wasn't doing well. Is she trying to blame him for not doing enough? Why talk to an unwilling parent? He saw enough of these types back in his village. Education just interfered with having free farm labor. He wanted her to think he at least cared about her Xin cousins and their education, but what was he supposed to do? He only survived by the good graces of her Uncle Xin. Frustration burrowed into his heart like maggots in a piece of meat.

"What do you think I should do? I can't pay for their supplies and the clan can't either," he said defensively. He couldn't hide his exasperation. His father had had so much less, with no clan school to help his son, yet he found a way to pay for a teacher, books, and ink. What was the matter with the boys' father? Did he not see the gift his clan gave his family, his boys?

"I think you might go talk to their father, that's all," she said. Her calm matched his impatience and indignation. "And perhaps the magistrate."

Shu-chang reeled on his heel. "The magistrate? What should I be talking to him about? I haven't' even met him, yet."

"He's head of the province and even though your school is a clan school, he's in charge of education. He might be able to find some solution; perhaps buy the school supplies. He's a northerner. They don't have clan schools as much up north. I heard their towns were more mixed with families from many different clans. Some towns had schools open to all able students, no matter which family they came from. So, given that he's from an area that supports early education for any able student, and since we've no such schools in our town using up town monies, he might do it."

"Maybe." Shu-chang groaned. What was this woman thinking? Still, as the boys' teacher, he felt responsible for them. "I don't see why their father can't buy ink," he tried one last time to extricate himself from more involvement, especially if it involved the magistrate.

"I visited their house last week. Their mother wasn't well," Xiang-hua said.

Shu-chang wiped his fingers over his forehead. "I'm sorry to hear that," he said, thinking that was one more reason for him to not visit the boys' home. Another expense, another reason not to come to school.

"She was quite ill."

He looked out the window. Maybe teaching Xiang-hua wasn't a good idea. Although it did give him a few extra coppers each month.

Xiang-hua went on, "She told me her husband's father had turned his land over to Master Gao many years ago as a tax protection. Her father-in-law paid Master Gao a relatively small fee in return for his being able to stay on the land and work it as his own."

Shu-chang stared at Xiang-hua. It was a familiar story. One that he knew too well from personal experience. He started to pay attention.

"Last year, San-fu demanded a much greater fee, even though it was a bad year for everyone's crops. Their father had managed to both pay and save his seed supply for the next season's planting. But this year was even worse. When San-fu demanded his fee, even a portion of the seed supply had to go." A ribbon of anger wove through her words. "They had to sell their daughter this spring in order to buy rice seedlings or they would have no food at all—and definitely nothing to give San-fu."

"Why is Master Gao allowing his grandson to behave this way?" Shu-chang asked.

"I don't know," she said. "I was called to San-fu's house the other day. Perhaps I can find out when I return."

"Well, there's no use in visiting the boys' family until after I've seen the magistrate," Shu-chang said.

Xiang-hua smiled.

Shu-chang looked away, then flipped a hand toward the desk. "We've wasted so much of your study time chatting, we won't be able to cover anything meaningful. Let's meet again next week when we can get down to work," he said gruffly.

Xiang-hua glanced around the empty room, a perplexed look on her face. Slowly she placed her writing implements back in the parcel, gave him a brief nod, and left.

He watched her. He felt guilty at cutting their lesson so short but not guilty enough to let her stay.

Shu-chang changed into a clean mourning robe and went to

see the magistrate. As the new teacher in town, it was proper for him to pay the magistrate a visit and introduce himself. As he prepared to go, he thought of Xiang-hua's pushing him to speak up for his students. This wasn't the time for such things, he mumbled to himself. How could he possibly bring up such a topic on his introductory trip to the magistrate's office? He pushed her concerns out of his mind. Uncle Xin had given him some delectable dried fruits from the Empire's western area. He had been saving them for a special occasion. Now they would be used as a gift for the magistrate.

Shu-chang didn't have to wait long before the magistrate's servant came to lead him into a large inner office, which the official had temporarily taken over while he stayed at the Gao home. The servant announced Shu-chang and, walking backwards, left the room.

Shu-chang stood in the open space before the magistrate. An impressive, robust man in his mid-40s, he sat in a heavy wooden chair. His hands lightly rested on its ornately carved arms. As Shu-chang was introduced, he leaned back into the chair.

"Teacher Hong Shu-chang, come and join me for a cup of tea."

Surprised and pleased by his greeting, Shu-chang approached quickly, stopped at the table before the magistrate, and bowed before sitting in the chair indicated.

"I hear you are teaching at the Xin clan school."

"Yes, Your Honor. It is small, but the students have promise," he said, the half-truth almost sticking in his throat.

"The town is fortunate to have such a distinctive teacher; you could have chosen a position in a much larger city with many more amenities, such as the provincial capital."

Shu-chang was again taken by surprise.

"Thank you, Sir. I am honored by your estimation of my poor abilities."

"Yes. Yes. I've just received a list of the top examination candidates and you were number one. Number one. Excellent. We'll have to have a small celebration to mark the occasion. You have brought great honor to the district. There has not been a notable candidate for many, many years."

Shu-chang was dumb-founded. He'd not only passed the examination, but he was number one! Overcome, he stopped breathing momentarily.

The magistrate watched him closely, then laughed, clapping his hands. "So, you hadn't heard the good news yet." He leaned forward. "You have suffered a great loss recently," he said delicately, referring to Shu-chang's father's and uncle's deaths, "but this shows that your fate is not all bad.

"Here, you must have some wine." And with that, the magistrate called his servant for wine and rice cakes.

After a couple of cups of the strong drink, and thinking about the magistrate's pleasure at his district's new status because of how well Shu-chang had done on the exams, the young teacher felt brave enough to bring up his school and its students' needs.

"... and so, you see, even though the students hold promise, their families are poor and with the crop failure of the past couple of years, even buying simple writing supplies is a problem," Shu-chang finished up, nervous about speaking forthrightly, yet anxious to get everything out once he'd started telling the story.

"Of course. Clan schools have done what they can, but it's not enough. I've been thinking that it's time for this town to have its own public school. It can be housed in the Bright Aura Temple until a proper building is built." He sat back and rubbed his hands together. "Your students can learn there. They'll also get supplies for their studies."

Such a scheme was perfect for solving the Xin clan's students' problems, but Shu-chang realized this also put him out of a job. Still, there wasn't any way he could deny them this opportunity. He put on a cheerful face. "Wonderful idea, Your Honor. Your generosity will bring honor to the town and to you."

"Of course, we will need the best teacher we can get." The magistrate stared at Shu-chang. "Perhaps you will consider taking the position. With adequate pay—plus a room to live in once the school is built."

Shu-chang bowed his appreciation, but did not agree, yet. Perhaps the magistrate was right: his fate wasn't all bad. This offer would give him a step up from his present position as teacher in the Xin clan's small school. At the same time, he was well aware of how his Uncle Xin and family came to his aid when he most needed it. For that, if for nothing else, he owed them his loyalty. At the same time, his present duties gave him time to study for the all-important third national examination and to carry out his duties toward his murdered father and his father's brother. Since the magistrate did not require an immediate response, Shu-chang remained silent.

Scrutinizing the young scholar's face, the magistrate finally nodded, and said: "Give it some thought."

Shu-chang bowed low once more, relieved—yet, also aware of how having more choices in his life created its own level of complications.

CHAPTER 9

Before Xiang-hua had finished knocking, the door to the Gao mansion opened; it was as if they were waiting for her. The servant immediately led her through to Madam Gao's rooms.

The family matriarch sat on a wooden platform surrounded by colorful, heavily embroidered cushions, which contrasted with her own dark, somber silk robe. The platform was bordered on three sides by an elaborately carved, lattice-like enclosure which rose to the ceiling. Seeing Xiang-hua, she placed the needlework project she was working on onto a simple, short-legged, and richly lacquered table in front of her. After greeting the young doctor warmly, she turned to her maid and ordered tea and snacks.

"Come. Sit," she said, indicating a high-backed chair near her platform.

Xiang-hua placed her bag on the floor next to the chair and sat. She admired the beauty in the room: the flowers artfully displayed in translucent porcelain vases and several long, vertical wall hangings of bamboo and peaceful rural, river scenes. On the opposite wall hung two of the most prominent scrolls, both on the virtues of filial piety. One, written in a strong, demanding script, admonished viewers to be careful in their behavior and to be frugal so that they are able to nourish their parents; the other was a painting of a son and daughter-in-law caring for his parents.

Madam Gao followed her gaze. "Those were wedding gifts from my in-laws. I cherish them. They remind us of our first duty in this life: supporting our parents and continuing the family line. It's our moral imperative."

Xiang-hua nodded. Sons owed filial piety to their parents and daughters owed filial piety to their parents-in-law. Once girls married, they were no longer considered an essential part of the natal family. An emotional bond may tie them to their own mother and father, but morally and legally they belonged only to their husband's family. Daughters-in-law were to produce sons to continue the family line and to care for their husband's parents.

Madam Gao turned her attention back to Xiang-hua, leaning toward her ever so slightly. "Tell me everything you've heard about the fire, Sister. Even the servants are excited about the events. Yet no one seems to be able to tell me much that makes sense." She made a face. "I've heard everything, including that a devil burned down our warehouse." At Xiang-hua's questioning look, she added: "As a punishment for my poor son's supposed transgressions against those lazy farmers who owe us money. Others claim a powerful gang did it." She smirked, "Although no one knows if any gang members actually exist in our town." She looked intently at Xiang-hua. "You go to so many houses; you must tell me what you've learned." With that, she waved to the maid who had just returned with a tray of tea and dried fruit to place it near her on the table. Picking up the tea pot, she filled their cups. and offered Xiang-hua a plate of dried fruit, she then settled back again and waited, expectation on her finely made-up face.

Xiang-hua accepted a cup of tea and took a sip as she collected her thoughts. She didn't want to tell Madam Gao anything about Xiao-ren, although she may already have heard rumors about him. She knew the older woman would be too tactful to mention Xiang-hua's brother's troubles to her.

"As you may have heard, Madam, the remains of two men were found in the rubble." Although she hadn't seen the bodies herself, she has seen severe burns and was well aware of the pain they caused. The idea of these men dying in the blazing building filled her with sympathy. "Such a tragedy. Their bodies were burnt beyond recognition. Apparently, two of the guards are missing, so right now the court believes they are the unfortunate victims."

"Ah. Because the warehouse is one of the Gao family's properties, I'm familiar with these men. Slightly, of course. They worked for San-fu for several years now. No wonder he's been so distracted these past two days." She drew her wide, silk sleeve up to her face and appeared to examine its colorfully embroidered flower motifs with some intensity. After a moment, she said: "There are several men working for him at the warehouse. Do you know the victims' names? San-fu will undoubtedly be arranging for their funerals."

"I'm sorry, Madam, they were not men I knew, nor were their families. I believe they were from the North, not from here."

She nodded. "And what caused the fire? The loss of a warehouse full of rice is a great economic tragedy for us and for the government."

"Because ...?"

"Why, most of that rice was what San-fu had collected as taxes. He's been the Emperor's tax collector for several years now; he took over that responsibility when his father passed away." She absently folded the hem of her sleeve back and forth. "He's such a hard worker."

Xiang-hua nodded, keeping her face a studied blank. Whoever collected taxes for the Emperor took a sizable percentage for himself. She wondered if there was any link between the fire and the building holding the year's supply of taxes owed the national government. Now there would be no way of telling what had been collected—or what had not. San-fu's ledgers would document who paid and how much, but that's all.

"Has anyone been arrested for the crime?" Madam Gao asked.

Xiang-hua squirmed on the wooden chair's flat seat, which felt uncommonly hard and unforgiving to her. "Not yet. He is still interviewing people. There was quite a long list of bystanders and possible witnesses. It's taking some time."

"But there must be some indication as to who did it," she persisted.

Xiang-hua let out a long sigh. "I'm afraid Xiao-ren is said to be involved."

"Oh, Sister! Such troubling circumstances for you and your family," Madam Gao sat up straighter, supporting herself with her right arm on the table as she bent toward Xiang-hua. She keenly searched the young woman's face.

"Indeed, it's a trying time." Xiang-hua tried to bury the anxiety that ate at her very being, hoping to hide her true feelings from herself as much as from her interlocutor.

"Where is he now? Is he at home?" She again discretely left out the bigger question of whether he was already in the hands of the court or not.

"He has not been home for two days."

"Did the soldiers ...?"

"He's not at court and he's not at home. Xiao-ren seems to have disappeared."

As matriarch of the family, Madam Gao was responsible for the entire household, its maintenance, and its people, therefore, Xiang-hua placed the daughter-in-law's medicine in her care. Finally, managing to extricate herself from the lady's interrogation, she left to attend to Erh-xi-fu.

On the way over to the sick woman's room, Xiang-hua questioned the maid about how well her mistress had been since she saw her last. The maid reported that she slept fitfully. She also ate little, although her mother-in-law had ordered that she have at least one meat dish and one egg each day. Still, she seemed to have no appetite.

When Xiang-hua entered the room, Madam Gao's daughter-in-law was sitting on an elevated wooden kang in the midst of a pile of colorfully embellished, silk pillows. A piece of untouched embroidery lay on her lap. The room and its decorations were a simplified version of her mother-in-law's room. Two scrolls hung from the wall facing the kang. One showed a young woman feeding an elderly woman and the other was a verse from the Book of Filial Piety. Both were admonitions to the daughter-in-law to care for her husband's parents.

"Sister, I am so glad you've come," Erh-xi-fu said. She was a delicate beauty with smooth, pale skin and black, thin eyebrows over clear, hematite eyes.

"Have you been taking the medicine I left for you?" Xiang-hua asked as she sat on the edge of the kang, close to her patient.

Erh-xi-fu nodded. "My mother-in-law comes to watch me personally when it is time for me to take it."

Xiang-hua grinned. The only way to get an heir was to care for the daughter-in-law and thereby make sure she conceives and successfully carries the fetus. Nevertheless, she noticed that Erh-xi-fu's demeanor was still depressed.

"Did San-fu come to your chambers last night?"

"Because you told Madam Gao he could not, he went to his first wife's room instead," she said. She slid her eyes toward the door. "He was not in a good mood. I heard him berate her severely."

Xiang-hua's chest tightened. She couldn't protect everyone who suffered. She stiffened her back; she would do what she could, one person at a time.

Xiang-hua felt Erh-xi-fu's pulse and nodded. "Your *qi* is still quite weak, but it's improving. Continue taking the medicine. I've given your mother-in-law the prescription, and please try to eat more. You must eat to recover."

"Sister, ... " Erh-xi-fu paused. "I will do as you say." Xiang-hua recognized an inconsistency between her words and her manner. She was certain the young wife still did not have the will to live and, without that, she could not get better.

"Erh-xi-fu, you can recover, but it is up to you. You are not fated to die so young."

The young wife hung her head. "What is the purpose of my recovering if my life is to be filled with pain I can't avoid, no matter what I do? My world is fine if San-fu comes home satisfied with his day or filled with retribution if his day was not good. It seems I am his relief for outside events. Events I can't control." Tears of frustration and unresolved anguish streamed down her cheeks. She turned her head away. "Forgive me for speaking out. It's wrong of me."

Xiang-hua took her hand. "You mustn't give in to despair. Even when things look impossible, we can't know what our fate is. Everyone has rough spots in their lives; no one escapes that. It doesn't mean this will last forever."

Erh-xi-fu stared at her, her eyes glistening with fresh tears. She whispered, "It's so hard. I don't know what to do."

"First of all, take care of yourself. The rest will follow," Xiang-hua said. It was all she could say.

When she left the ailing young woman, Xiang-hua hoped that her words of encouragement were true. Living with such a brutal husband and an uncaring mother-in-law was a dangerous combination.

After leaving the Gao compound, Xiang-hua quickly marched a couple of blocks down the street. Stopping at a plain, weather-worn door set off on a side road, she adjusted the parcel on her shoulder and knocked.

A high-pitched, quivering voice bade her enter.

She stepped into the dark, one-room house. A wizened woman with her hair pulled back flat against her head was sitting with her legs tucked under her on a brick kang that took up most of the tiny interior. She lifted her head in greeting and started to rise. Her smiling, wrinkled face could not hide the anxiety Xiang-hua read in her furrowed brow.

Xiang-hua quickly put a hand up. "Please, don't get up, Grandmother," she said, showing respect by using the honorific for the old woman.

The elder relaxed and remained seated near a large pot of greens she'd been preparing for the evening meal. "Sister, I'm so glad you could come. How is your grandmother, Yi-po?"

"She would certainly have come to see your daughter-in-law, but she is at the provincial capital on a mission. She will visit you when she returns," Xiang-hua said. She was well aware that clients expected her to be assisting her grandmother and were surprised at her coming alone.

"The provincial capital! Ah! What an honor. And she

deserves it. Her doctoring skills are famous throughout the region. As yours will be," she added grinning benignly at the young medical doctor.

"You are too kind," Xiang-hua said. "Is your daughter-in-law home?"

"She's here." And the woman shifted allowing Xiang-hua to see the rest of the platform she sat on. The kang was the family's sleeping and working space. A figure lay unmoving on a straw mat which had been rolled out over the kang's brick foundation. A fire in the brick stove built into the room's corner warmed the tiny room. A thin congee, a rice soup, cooked gently in a pot—nourishment for her daughter-in-law.

Xiang-hua stepped beside the old woman. She cast a glance at the figure on the brick kang: a plump woman in her early twenties lay on her side, her swollen belly covered with a light cloth, her ample breasts exposed.

"How are you doing, Lotus?" Xiang-hua asked.

"It will be soon," she said.

Xiang-hua nodded. Lotus should give birth within the next week. But that was not why Xiang-hua was here. A mid-wife would come to help deliver the baby.

After a few pleasantries, Xiang-hua turned to the older woman. "Let's sit near the door."

They took two stools and settled at the entrance, where the overcast day allowed a weak light to penetrate the room. Xiang-hua sat close to the older woman, took her wrist, monitored her pulse for a short time, and then placed the hand back on the woman's lap.

"You should have called me sooner," Xiang-hua admonished.

"I know you're busy," she replied.

Xiang-hua suspected that she really didn't want to spend money on herself when her daughter-in-law was so close to giving birth and the mid-wife had to be paid for her services.

Xiang-hua looked at the wrinkled face of the woman before her. She appeared to be in her late sixties, but Xiang-hua knew she was in her early fifties. A hard life had taken its toll, yet she remained an optimistic, cheerful person. Xiang-hua admired her strength and fortitude.

After prescribing medicine, Xiang-hua said, "You will also need a round of moxibustion treatments. I'll return tomorrow to give you the first one."

"As you say."

Looking out of the doorway, Xiang-hua said, "You're quite close to the warehouses that burned. Did you happen to see anyone who looked suspicious or out of place that day?"

"I may have. There are so many people on the streets nowadays, not like it used to be when I knew everyone." She pursed her lips. "Then again, my eyes aren't what they used to be either." She grinned toothlessly. "But I'm sure I didn't see your Xiao-ren. I always know him."

Xiang-hua breathed a sigh of relief. Her fear was that someone would say they had seen him and at just the wrong time. Keeping her voice even, she asked, "Why is that? Are you certain?"

"Oh, yes. He always wears a red cloth around his waist and he's a strapping boy with a dodgy walk." She shot a look at Xiang-hua. "Oh, sorry. I didn't mean that. It's just that he always looks like he's about to take off, run away. You know what I mean."

Unfortunately, Xiang-hua did. For all his bravado and cockiness, her younger brother had the perpetual look of a puppy about to be reprimanded. Probably because he was always up to something he shouldn't be, she mused.

Xiang-hua patted the elder woman's arm. "It's all right. He can be a handful. But you're sure you didn't see him around the warehouse district that day?"

"I'm as sure as I can be. Come to think of it, there did

seem to be a lot of activity very early in the morning. Sacks of rice were being moved. But it's a warehouse. You'd expect men to be moving rice in or out almost all the time. And it's time to transport the Emperor's rice to the capital."

Leaving the house, Xiang-hua mulled over their conversation. Yes, she was relieved to hear that her brother hadn't been seen in the area around the time of the fire, yet she worried. The older woman had said that her eyes were not as good as they used to be. Could she have simply not recognized him, in spite of her certainty? And, if he really wasn't there, why did some of the other locals say he was?

-

CHAPTER 10

Shu-chang held the bowl of congee to his lips and slurped. The thick, creamy porridge slipped down his throat and warmed his stomach. Early morning sunlight filtered through the open window. In spite of the streaming sunbeams, the day already looked dreary to Shu-chang. He watched his uncle pick up a small pickle with his chopsticks and place it in his mouth. Neither spoke; only the guzzling and crunching of their breakfast could be heard.

His uncle had been out late last night, so Shu-chang hadn't had a chance to talk to him about his visit to the magistrate. He didn't know what Uncle Xin would think of having a new public school. Of course, it might be good for the town, but would he want his own clan students to attend when they now had their own school? And then there was the possibility that Shu-chang would leave the clan school and teach at the public school, with its better salary and his own place to live.

He decided to leave that conversation for this evening, after he returned from class.

"Did Chu find his son," Shu-chang asked.

Xin frowned. "No. He's probably staying with friends. Afraid to come home. Afraid the court will arrest him. Or at least take him in for questioning." His sentences came ragged and fast. He placed his chopsticks down on the table. "His absence makes him look even more guilty. Everyone is talking about it. There's no way to avoid being interviewed by the court."

Shu-chang had very little knowledge or experience with the law. Any infractions in his small village were taken care of by the elders. They had had no serious crimes. Not until recently, he thought glumly. But even his father and uncle's murder case brought little from the courts. So, this kind of situation caused by the warehouse fire and the double deaths were new to him. Still, even he understood the implications of hiding from the court—especially when the tide of gossip was against you. Surely the magistrate heard the same rumors.

His behavior is jeopardizing the whole family," Shu-chang said.

Xin nodded, his face grim. "We will continue looking for him today."

"Do you think he left the town, maybe the district?"

"Where would he go? He has no money, no contacts that we know of. He doesn't have permission to travel. Even a journey to the next largest town or city would prove hazardous to him."

"So he must be here somewhere," Shu-chang said.

As they turned over the day's plan to find Xiao-ren, Chu rushed into the room.

"The soldiers found Xiao-ren last night and are holding him," Chu said breathlessly.

"Where was he? How did they find him? How long have they had him? What do you hear from the courts?" Xin asked, his questions tumbling over each other.

"Apparently, someone tipped off the soldiers that he was hiding out on the north side of town. They found him late last night sleeping in a small grove of bamboo. He was alone." Chu vigorously rubbed his head. "I heard from one of the court runners that he's being held until the magistrate gets to him late this afternoon for questioning."

"That's not good," Xin said. "We need to gift the jailer as soon as possible."

Although Shu-chang barely knew Xiao-ren, and only then as a troublesome and disrespectful student, his stomach tightened at the thought of his cousin being tortured. He'd understood the law forbade serious torture for minors, but he was not sure Xiao-ren would be considered a minor. At sixteen, had he already passed into the age of adulthood? Shu-chang didn't know the law well enough. Then, too, often things happened in jail that weren't legal. Giving a gift to the jailer gave some assurance that the arrested person would have an added, and needed, layer of protection against "accidents." Often prison officers used the threat of torture to extract money and other "gifts" from the accused's relatives. So, no matter what the law decreed, it was imperative for the family to cobble together as much as they could to give the various guards and jailers who could do harm to Xiao-ren while he was in custody.

"We don't need something big and expensive—yet. A special tea will take care of it. We just want everyone, the guards and warden, on our side through today. I'll go for you." Xin said. He stood. "Let's hope the magistrate lets him go after questioning, but we must be prepared. We'll need a bigger and more impressive gift if the magistrate decides to keep him as a suspect."

Chu's face turned gray. He grabbed Shu-chang's hand. "You must help him. You must find out who really set the fire and killed those men."

Shu-chang bowed slightly toward Chu. "I'll do my best."

Nevertheless, unspoken questions ran through his mind: *What am I to do? I'm an outsider. Who would trust me? Why don't they do it themselves?* Even though he felt guilty and unthankful when the last question popped into his mind, he couldn't help but wonder.

As if noticing the young man's discomfort, Uncle Xin said, "You have great stature in the town. You're a teacher and you've passed the second level of exams, so you're not only a *juren*, but the *jieyuan*, the one who ranked first in the provincial examination. You're the first jieyuan this district has produced in many, many years."

Xin grinned in response to Shu-chang's obvious surprise that he'd heard about his nephew's passing.

"Nothing can be kept hidden long. The magistrate is arranging a ceremony to honor your success. If you ask people questions they will be pleased to speak to you. Being seen with you, and being in your presence—at least for the next few days—gives them status. You can use it to our advantage in finding out more about the warehouse," Xin said.

"I'll do my best," Shu-chang repeated, feeling over-whelmed with a mix of pride and responsibility.

Spectators filled the Gao's courtyard beyond its ample capacity. They'd come to hear the magistrate question each of the witnesses. There were so many viewers in attendance, they spilled out into the streets. Unable to personally watch the proceedings, they comforted themselves by buying street food, which was readily available from the gathered peddlers' carts.

Shu-chang breathed in the inviting fragrance of peppers, onions, and soy sauce that permeated the air outside the courtyard before plunging into the crowd behind Chu and Xin. They pushed their way through the packed audience and slowly made their way into the main enclosure. Some in the crowd moved aside as they approached, but others ignored them and wouldn't give way. Chu elbowed through the men standing shoulder to shoulder, making a path for Xin and Shu-chang to follow. The crush of people meant sweat and body odor soon replaced the pleasant cooking aromas outside the compound.

Although the questioning took place in the Gao compound's courtyard, the power and authority of the court was clear. The magistrate wore a dark robe with his official insignia of a large, ornately embroidered square patch of a brilliant bird in flight prominently resting on his chest. His stiff black, gauze hat with oval-shaped, black wings on either side also announced his position of authority. He sat in a high-backed chair, behind a massive and heavily carved elm table polished a deep brown.

Eventually, Shu-chang, Uncle Xin, and Chu made it to the front of the masses and stood, waiting. The questioning of all those who might have seen anything had been going on for some time already. They arrived just as another bystander was finishing his testimony. Apparently, he'd not been able to offer any solid information. However, before he was dismissed, he added, without the judge's prompting, that he'd heard Xiao-ren was there. Then, looking out into the audience and catching a glimpse of Chu, he quickly added that he wasn't certain, but he'd heard it from several people.

The court's secretary sitting at a table off to the side, carefully noted his deposition. Shu-chang's heart sank as he watched the brush fly across the secretary's paper.

The magistrate excused the interviewee and called for the next bystander. This went on for two more people until, finally, the group of bystanders had all been interviewed. The magistrate called out, "Bring Xin Xiao-ren, son of Xin Chu, for questioning."

A rumble went through the crowd as a soldier went to fetch him.

"Silence!" A guard commanded. The general volume decreased, but a constant underlying grumbling remained. By this time, the community was coming to the decision about Xiao-ren's guilt. Xin stood to the left of Chu and Shu-chang to the right. Once people felt Xiao-ren was the perpetrator, an explosion of vigilante justice was more than possible. With that, the young man's entire family could be held accountable, including his father. Justice demanded collective responsibility for a crime and the crowd was more than willing to administer their own brand of punishment.

The crowd didn't have to wait long before Xiao-ren was led before the magistrate. He looked haggard and filthy. Dirt clung to his sweaty face and neck. He could barely walk; his guard had to prod him forward. Xiao-ren limped and stumbled toward the judge.

"Oh, my son," Chu mumbled in anguish as he stared at the young man's halting and unsteady progress through the courtyard and toward the magistrate' bench. Clearly the gifts to the jailer had not come soon enough. Xiao-ren had already been at the receiving end of some very rough handling, if not outright torture.

A surge of pity rose up in Shu-chang as he watched his student advance with a hobbling gait. By law, torture was required if a criminal refused to own up to his crimes. Confession showed a moral acceptance of his responsibility and was a necessary part of the judicial process. But that part of the law was to be applied only at the stage when the judge felt sure the person was, in fact, the guilty party. Raising the question of why Xiao-ren had received such rough treatment already. Shu-chang was certain the case hadn't gotten to that stage. Not yet.

Xiao-ren bowed before the judge.

"Two great crimes have been committed," the magistrate began sternly, "the willful burning of a warehouse holding government property and the resultant deaths of two innocent men. Tell the court your role in these crimes," he commanded.

Xiao-ren's voice shook as he answered. "Honorable Sir, I know nothing. I was in the back of The Golden Pheasant bar when the warehouse burned and the men died."

"If this is so, who are your witnesses? Who saw you at The Golden Pheasant bar?"

Xiao-ren hung his head. "No one, Your Honor. I was alone. No one saw me, but I was there. I'm telling the truth."

"Stop deceiving the court! If you confess now, I can be lenient with you. Otherwise the court will come down on you with its full force," the judge yelled.

Xiao-ren collapsed to the floor.

Chu started forward, but Xin and Shu-chang held him back just as a soldier was about to push him away with a spear.

"Confess!" the judge yelled again.

Xiao-ren slowly raised his head. "I was not there. I didn't do anything."

As if exasperated, the judge leaned toward the young man. "This is your last chance."

Xiao-ren hung his head and said nothing.

"Take him back to jail. Perhaps he will confess after giving his crimes more thought," the judge commanded. That was a command to use torture as needed to force a guilty plea.

Chu's legs gave way and he fell back into the arms of Xin and Shu-chang.

CHAPTER 11

Xiang-hua crushed dried herbs in a long-used stone mortar as her grandmother had instructed before she left. Some of the herbs would be mixed with others to alleviate stomach problems; some would be kept in a small jar to be used as needed in other concoctions or on their own.

The aroma of the newly pulverized herbs, mixed with the others in the room, gave her a sense of peace. Ever since she was a young child, she had spent many an hour here with her grandmother doing simple tasks and learning about the various herbs. Her grandmother, and sometimes her grandfather, taught her to read and write. Her grandfather was well known within the regional literary circle for his brilliance, and he encouraged his grandchildren, both Xiang-hua and Xiao-ren, to embrace the classics as well as the tales his fellow scholars loved to write and share. These were stories of foxes and spirits. Some were cautionary fables—behave or there will be retribution of one sort or another—while others reveled in the wonder of mystical happenings. When she was small, he allowed her to sit in the room as he and his friends discussed such tales and their merits.

She had always loved those evenings. Xiao-ren, however, was another matter. Reading bored him; the only literary pursuits he enjoyed were such books as the *Water Margin Stories,* a heroic tale written in the vernacular about 108 outlaws and their daring, fearless adventures. He also devoured Sun-tzu's *The Art of War*, a book on military strategy. Their father allowed him to take martial arts training only because the Emperor still insisted that even the literati be able to protect the country from attacks by barbarians.

As her hands gently pounded the dried leaves into a fine powder, a shadow darkened the workbench.

"Xiang-hua," her father said, "you're up late."

"I need medicine for a patient tomorrow," she said. "Are you all right?" Normally her father never came into her work area. He had not embraced medicine; instead he had shown exceptional ability in business. While his own father and mother were well-known doctors in the region, he ran the family's pharmaceutical shop, which was now larger than even those at the provincial capital.

Chu rubbed his eyes. "Yes. No. It's Xiao-ren."

Xiang-hua stopped grinding the pestle against the mortar, and waited. She was afraid to hear what he had to say, fearing bad news about her brother, and, at the same time, needing to know.

"I've just returned from the courts. The magistrate interviewed Xiao-ren today." He dropped his head, then looked up at her. "It did not go well."

Xiang-hua exhaled, letting out a long breath she didn't know she was holding.

"The magistrate wanted him to confess to arson. That would mean he'd be confessing to killing the two men. He refused. Of course, he did. He's innocent." As he said this, his voice hardened.

She nodded her head. If he had confessed, he might be

given a lighter sentence because of his young age, but his father—their father—would still be held accountable and guilty of the crime. Chu was responsible for his son and his behavior, therefore, he could be given the maximum sentence possible under the law. Death and the state's seizure of all his land and property. Making his family destitute. The ramifications of Xiao-ren's involvement made Xiang-hua's head spin.

"Pa..."

"Because he refused to confess, the magistrate ordered him back to jail. He will be interviewed again tomorrow."

Xiang-hua felt faint and reached out to her bench for support. Overnight her family's life had turned upside down.

"We need to make sure Xiao-ren is safe until the real criminals are found," she said, not wanting to mention the word torture. That would be bad luck.

"Uncle Xin is helping. He's raising *guanxi*, gifts to smooth out relationships between people, from the clan. We will need a lot: for the jailers, but also for the runners, the court recorder, so many others—not to mention *guanxi* for the magistrate." He pushed against the bridge of his nose and stared at the mortar.

Xiang-hua pursed her lips. "Do you think the magistrate will really look further than Xiao-ren for the criminals? He is a handy scapegoat for the crime."

"It's uncertain at this time," her father said, his words catching in his throat.

"We must do something."

"Shu-chang promised to investigate. People will open up to him—especially now that he's a local celebrity."

Xiang-hua threw him a quizzical glance.

"Ah, you've been working here in your lab and haven't heard. Shu-chang passed the provincial examination at the highest level; he was number one, the *jie-yuan*. Even Shu-chang didn't know until the magistrate told him. My sister can be proud of her son." Chu allowed himself a chuckle picturing his sister in the netherworld celebrating her son's achievement. Then he grew serious again. "We're hoping he can mingle with people in the tea and wine shops to find out who was involved in any way. Perhaps even discover who did this terrible thing."

"I can help, too," Xiang-hua said. All day, as she worked, she had been mulling over where she could ferret out information. Which clients' houses she could call on.

Her father smiled. "Yes. You have the ear of many a housewife. They know what their husbands are up to and they might tell you. Wonderful."

"I'll be leaving momentarily, and I'll visit as many families as I can. Do you have any idea who I should see in particular?"

Chu rubbed his nose again. "You should talk to Shu-chang about that. He spent time gossiping with runners and jailers at court after the proceeding. He may already have a list of people to check further.

"If he's not at Uncle Xin's, he'll return shortly. I'll ask him to join us this evening."

Neither of them mentioned the danger their immediate family and the Xin clan could very well be in, if Xiao-ren was found guilty. They didn't have to.

It turned out that Shu-chang had returned, so he and Uncle Xin were able to join Chu and Xiang-hua after only a brief interlude.

It only took a glance at Shu-chang for Xiang-hua to read the stress and discouragement in his body.

"Tell us what you've learned so far," Uncle Xin said as Shu-chang folded himself onto a chair. He had managed to hold off asking his nephew questions until all of them were together, but his impatient tugging on his sleeves showed he could wait no longer.

"It's a good thing we were able to give the jailer a gift early on," Shu-chang said. "It made giving him another small gift easier." He reached into his sleeve and pulled out a piece of paper. "Here's a list of the people that we will have to gift and at what levels I think would be appropriate."

Chu took the list and blanched. It was not short. He handed it over to Xin.

Xin carefully examined the list. "I believe we can cover this. I have promises from several other Xin families already."

Xiang-hua remained silent. She hoped Uncle Xin wasn't being too optimistic. Many families in their clan were on the brink of collapse. This would be difficult for the entire extended family. If found guilty, there was not only the deaths of two unimportant men to consider, but the destruction of the Emperor's yearly taxes. And the latter was one of the greatest crimes that could be committed because it was against the state and its ability to govern successfully. The Emperor and his men would certainly bring the full force of the law against the entire Xin clan. Collective responsibility didn't stop with a person's parents; it included the family network over many generations.

"The bad news is that unless we get a break, it will be extremely difficult to find the perpetrators," Shu-chang said. "I talked to several people in the know at court. At this point, only Xiao-ren is mentioned as a possible suspect. There is no one else."

"How could a boy of sixteen do such a thing? He wouldn't even be able to purchase the supplies he'd need to set such a fire. And why wouldn't he have a friend—anybody—vouch that he was someplace else at the time?" Chu exploded. "He's not that manipulative. He always acts before he thinks."

"Please don't say that outside of this room," Uncle Xin said. "They will say he torched the place out of uncontrolled anger. Remember, some are saying he was angry with San-fu."

Chu rapidly rubbed his hand through his hair as if trying to get rid of this nightmare.

Xiang-hua coughed to bring their attention to her. As the youngest and only female in the room, she was not supposed to boldly offer her opinion without being asked for it. Uncle Xin looked at her. Her father nodded as if remembering something important. His eyes brightened.

"Oh, yes. Shu-chang, Xiang-hua has access to many of the households in the village because she treats female aliments. Sometimes women talk when their men won't, if you get what I mean."

Shu-chang nodded, but Xiang-hua didn't miss the slight tightening of his mouth.

"If you tell me which families you would like to learn more about, I could visit them in my rounds," she said, ready to argue with him if need be.

But then he surprised her with: "That's a great idea. It's much like Sun-tsu's pincher movement in *The Art of War*."

Xiang-hua grinned. It's just the kind of thing her brother would have said.

CHAPTER 12

A bitter wind rushed through the streets, stirring up a mixture of dust and the smell of freshly cooked food sold by petty merchants with hand carts. Xiang-hua's outer coat flapped hard against her legs. Head down against bursts of dust, she grasped her medicine bag close to her body with her right hand and firmly clasped her large brimmed hat onto her head with the other.

"Sister, how good to see you on such a windy day."

Xiang-hua stopped and looked up to see Granny standing an arm's length away. She had almost run right into her.

"And good to see you, too, Granny. Is there to be a birth today?" Granny was the most sought-after mid-wife in the area.

Granny shook her head. "The winemaker's daughter is to be engaged soon, so his wife commissioned me to find some items for the girl's dowry. I've been visiting many of the merchants, particularly those across from the warehouses. Lots of jewelers work along that street," she added, giving Xiang-hua a long look.

Xiang-hua took the hint. "Ah, from what I understand,

none of them have been interviewed by the magistrate about the warehouse incident because they hadn't been in the crowd at the time of the fire."

Granny grinned and nodded. "The magistrate didn't throw his net far enough in looking for informants.

"One merchant, who I won't name, told me this story: It turns out that if the Emperor's inspector had gotten into the warehouse before the fire, he would have found a lot more rice had been collected as tax than had been recorded."

Xiang-hua pursed her lips, then said, "How could he possibly know that? Was it one of Master Gao's accountants?"

Granny threw her hands up in the air. "No, but I can't say who told me. He had heard this from other people. People in the know." She winked.

"That's not good, but from what my father says, just about every possibility has been discussed by the men in the wine shops. Your source could simply be repeating hearsay and nothing more. He's suggesting that San-fu collected more taxes than what the Emperor actually required, and he would illegally gain by keeping the difference." She struggled with the bag under her arm as the wind suddenly grabbed it. Settling it back against her side, she continued. "That would be hard to prove. Besides, excess rice paid in taxes could simply have been removed before the inspector arrived. That can't have been difficult."

"Apparently, the inspector arrived without warning; there was no time to remove the rice." Granny's greying hair flew around her face. She tried to hold it down, but to no avail.

"Hum. So, while San-fu normally keeps a small percentage of the tax he collects, this would be defrauding the Emperor and a serious crime." She stared at Granny. "But then, so is burning down His Majesty's warehouse. The crime would merit the death penalty for arson against the government, not to mention the two deaths."

"Dire only if found guilty," Granny said.

The implications were not lost on Xiang-hua. "A sixteen-year-old boy couldn't defraud the government of its rightful share of the taxes, but he could be found to recklessly and vengefully set fire to the warehouse, which coincidently destroyed evidence of how much rice had actually been collected from the people. I must alert Shu-chang right away so that he can inform the magistrate," Xiang-hua said, starting to turn to leave.

"Wait. There's more to consider."

Irritated at losing time while her brother may be being tortured, Xiang-hua impatiently turned back.

"Another merchant, who I have also found to be reliable in the past, had another plausible story. As we've seen over the past many months, there's a daring new gang in the region, which has the uncanny ability to know when and where to rob traveling merchants. Traveling merchants with expensive goods. The fellow I talked to said he thought they had men working in key areas, such as at the various warehouses. The gang's henchmen learn a lot by listening and watching. That information is passed along to their boss, who then decides which shipments to rob for the greatest profit."

"Sounds plausible."

"However, the guards at the warehouse holding the rice were nervous. Any crime against the government could lead to the death sentence. They wanted to quit. Their boss wouldn't let them. They threatened to tell the magistrate about the gang's activities and who was involved, so they had to be silenced. They were killed and the fire was set to hide the fact that their deaths weren't from other causes."

"Did your merchant informer tell you who these gang members are?" Xiang-hua asked.

"He couldn't, or wouldn't, say."

"Did any of the other merchants corroborate either of these stories?"

"All of the others claimed to know only what everyone on the street was saying. They had no new ideas or information," Granny said.

Xiang-hua chewed her lip. "Well, if it's a tax issue, we'd be looking at San-fu; if it's a gang issue, we have to dig into who the members are and who their leader is."

"I'll continue visiting the merchants as I look for the dowry gifts," Granny said.

"Thank you so much for uncovering all of this." The wind died down momentarily and Xiang-hua opened her medicine bag. "By the way, I was grinding mugwort last night and I have more than I need. Please take a bag of it."

Granny eagerly snatched the bag, carefully opened it, and poked her finger into the powder. "It is kind of you to think of me," she said, closing the bag and tucking it into her sleeve.

As Granny left, Xiang-hua again tucked her medicine bag under her arm. Now she would have to return to her lab and fetch more mugwort. She needed it for Erh-xi-fu's treatment.

And she could also tell her father about her conversation with Granny.

Xiang-hua heard voices coming from the house before she entered. She recognized the first, more excited one as her father's, but was less sure of the identity behind the lower, more controlled responses. She entered the room and saw her father, Uncle Xin, and Shu-chang clustered together in an earnest discussion.

"What did you find out today?" her father greeted her.

"We need to act quickly or, before your brother is released, he'll be crippled for life."

"We are doing all that is possible, Chu," Xin said, his voice tense.

"We have already arranged for *guanxi* to be spread among the necessary people," Shu-chang said.

Chu ignored their remarks, his eyes searching Xiang-hua's face for hints of her success.

"I have news. I talked with Granny. She's been visiting the merchants along the warehouse street and has discovered some more information—what it's worth, I can't say."

"We'll determine that," her father said.

Xiang-hua repeated everything Granny said and emphasized that the two possible alternate scenarios were told to her by only one person each. And both were vague with no real names or even identifying characteristics to help them determine who could be involved.

"This is something, but not enough," her father said when she finished.

"It's like smoke in the night," Uncle Xin said. "Besides, if we accuse San-fu, he'll say that we're trying to frame him and the Gao clan because of a grudge. And don't forget that his grandfather is still alive. As a successful candidate in the national exams he and his family are protected under the law. We would have to have an unbreakable case against him."

Xiang-hua scrunched her nose, frustrated at the truth in his comments. Yet, she believed she had come up with some real paths to follow.

"This information can help." Shu-chang said. He stood up and paced around the room. "I'll follow up on these two possible scenarios. They appear to support some other rumblings I heard when I was in the crowd watching the flames take the warehouse." He sat back down, crossed his arms, and tapped his chin. He looked over at them. "I can look into the tea and wine shops. Men often have loose lips when drinking." He smiled grimly. "Granny is checking the merchants; Xiang-hua is able to get into the Gao mansion and talk to the women there."

Xiang-hua glanced at him. He frowned as he spoke, drawing his black eyebrows together like a bird in flight. He looked up and nodded. "By working together, we'll bring Xiao-ren safely home."

She nodded in return, but a nagging sensation ate at her stomach. Would it be soon enough?

CHAPTER 13

Xiang-hua once again entered the Gao mansion and was led through the courtyards and down several verandas to Mistress Gao, who greeted her enthusiastically.

"My son tells me he saw you on the streets earlier today talking with Granny." She grinned. "'Two trouble-makers meeting,' he said." She laughed as she laid her embroidery aside. "Now don't take offense. You know men; they always think that when women get together, trouble will follow." She giggled. "But I know what he means. Without you two, most of us wouldn't know what's happening in the outside world at all, which might make our men quite happy." She tapped the chair next to her. "Never mind. Come, sit. Tell me how things are progressing on this awful warehouse affair. Poor San-fu has been irritable and grumpy ever since it's happened. Being responsible for the Emperor's taxes is a big responsibility. This is a disaster for him."

Xiang-hua sat and waited until Mistress Gao finished ordering the maid to bring tea and rice cakes. Once the maid left, Xiang-hua bent closer to Mistress Gao.

"I did hear through Granny that it looks like the fire was set by gang members."

Mistress Gao's hand flew to her mouth, covering it.

"Oh, how terrible. But why would they want to destroy the Emperor's property? It's such a dangerous thing to do; it's sure to bring His Majesty's wrath down on them." She picked up a fan and rapidly flicked it back and forth creating a wind storm. Xiang-hua unconsciously leaned away slightly from the sudden burst of air.

"I'm so sorry to hear that Xiao-ren is mixed up with such a gang. It must be an awful blow to your father."

Xiang-hua stared at her momentarily, digesting Mistress Gao's meaning.

"No. I didn't mean Xiao-ren is involved with a gang. If we can find this gang or at least one of its members, Xiao-ren will be absolved of all involvement."

Mistress Gao held her eyes. "You want to believe in your brother, Sister. That's only natural. I hope you're right."

Xiang-hua pushed the rising anger that was filling her chest. She had to remind herself to stay on track, to get information from San-fu's mother.

"Whoever is found guilty of arson, your honorable father-in-law has to be upset. Would you like me to give him a sedative to help him rest? At his age, such news could be overwhelming and that would be bad for his health."

Mistress Gao smirked and shook her head. "That's kind of you, Sister, but San-fu's grandfather is not in the least bit concerned."

Xiang-hua raised her eyebrows in surprise.

Mistress Gao picked out a rice cake and delicately bit into it. "These are not bad. Please have one."

At that, her maid picked up the plate and offered it to Xiang-hua, who took one and held it over her lap.

"Don't be surprised about my father-in-law," Mistress Gao said, replacing the cake and brushing her fingers to get rid of the crumbs. "He's become senile; he lives in the past. In his glory days." She shifted in her chair. "San-fu has taken over everything. If it weren't for him, the house of Gao would be dust."

"So that means ...," Xiang-hua began.

"Yes. You mustn't tell anyone. I'll hold you accountable," she said, and the look in her steely, cold eyes told Xiang-hua she meant it.

"It is necessary for the good of the family that San-fu assume the role of head of household. But, of course, no one can know that his grandfather's senile and not capable of making rational decisions. He stays in his rooms. He's quite comfortable; I take care of him."

"What about your father-in-law's official duties?" Xiang-hua finally asked.

"Oh, that's easy. San-fu has his grandfather's chop."

"You're saying San-fu assumes his grandfather's identity in signing official papers?"

"Oh, no, it's not like that. My son is merely carrying out his grandfather's duties. As Master Gao would wish. After all, my father-in-law has both represented the town to the Emperor and represented the Emperor's government to its citizens for more than 40 years. We in the family understand his work. It is as if San-fu is his grandfather's hands and eyes."

Xiang-hua thought of the many area farmers who were losing their fields to San-fu's greed and wondered if he was indeed his grandfather's eyes and hands. He certainly wasn't his ears, since he didn't hear the farmers' pain.

Eventually, the conversation turned to the ostensible reason Xiang-hua was at the mansion: to care for Erh-xi-fu. Mistress Gao seemed uninterested in the topic and called one of her maids into the room.

"You've been serving San-fu's second wife. Please tell Sister how she is progressing."

"She takes the medicine Madam has given my Mistress. She has been eating better and keeping the food down. I haven't seen her vomit since your last visit." The maid reported succinctly.

"And what about her sleep?" Xiang-hua asked.

"She still sleeps in fits. Troubled dreams wake her with a start."

Mistress Gao sneered. "She is a lot of trouble, as you can see. Please do all you can to make sure she will produce a son for the Gao family. The first wife proved worthless; our hopes are now on her."

Xiang-hua held her irritation in check. Obviously, there was no concern for Erh-xi-fu herself. To the Gao family, she was merely a vehicle for delivering a descendent. Not very kind, but useful to Xiang-hua in getting them to comply with the treatment she'd recommend for Erh-xi-fu.

Xiang-hua pulled out a large cone of mugwort along with two small packages and placed them on a table next to Erh-xi-fu's kang. The young woman watched her with curiosity. She lay with her smooth belly exposed, the silk of her clothing folded back and bunched around her waist and hips.

Opening one of the packages, Xiang-hua said, "This is the medicine I'll give your mother-in-law for you." She tapped the second package. "These are my needles for doing acupuncture, but today," she reached for the cone of mugwort and held it up, "I only want to use the moxibustion technique."

"I haven't heard of that before," Erh-xi-fu said, and

quickly added, "Of course, I completely trust whatever you do."

Xiang-hua had a maid bring a small fire over and lit the fat cone. It took a short time for the cone to catch fire and burn on its own.

Erh-xi-fu watched her prepare for the moxibustion heat therapy. Her growing concern clearly visible in a narrowing of her eyes and a tightening of her lips.

Xiang-hua looked up at her patient. "This is something my grandmother has been working on for many, many years. It is a special therapy technique for women who can't get pregnant," Xiang-hua said quietly, still she couldn't keep the note of pride out of her voice. Moxibustion was an ancient technique, going back hundreds and hundreds of years, but they were refining it and, hopefully, improving and expanding its usefulness. She wanted Erh-xi-fu to feel comfortable, to believe this treatment was essential to combat her illness.

The young wife nodded and looked away.

As Xiang-hua moved closer to the young woman and started to bring the burning cone to her stomach, however, Erh-xi-fu unconsciously pulled back.

"Lie still. I'm not going to burn you," Xiang-hua said sternly. "This won't hurt."

Erh-xi-fu closed her eyes and stopped moving, her hands clenched at her sides.

Slowly Xiang-hua began moving the burning cone just over the top of Erh-xi-fu's abdomen. She started at her navel first moving in an ever-enlarging circle, and then from side to side across her stomach. Every now and then, she'd pause and remove the ash which built up at the end of the cone. She didn't want hot ash to fall on her client's tender skin.

"How do you feel?"

"Warm and comfortable."

"Good. I'll come each day for a week. This will release your pent-up energies and open your meridians."

Xiang-hua extinguished the moxa cone and placed it in a dish, letting it cool. She pulled the silken garment over the woman's bare skin.

Erh-xi-fu started to rise.

"Stay lying down; rest a while."

They sat together in silence.

"Do you believe in fate?" Erh-xi-fu asked.

"I believe we must do all we can to help ourselves and those around us," Xiang-hua said. "Otherwise, why do we have medicines? We could just wait for our fate to cure or kill us."

Erh-xi-fu smiled ruefully at her young doctor. "Perhaps their success is up to fate. Your grandmother is experimenting with this technique, but maybe it works only if her patient is fated to get better or to have a child."

"I can't agree with that. How could I be a doctor if I didn't believe in the ability of medicines and medical techniques to cure or at least help people survive terrible illnesses? As it is, I've already heard and seen many amazing recoveries."

Erh-xi-fu closed her eyes and lay quietly until her breathing became slow and regular. She'd fallen asleep.

Xiang-hua noiselessly gathered her materials, gave the medicine to the maid to take over to Erh-xi-fu's mother-in-law, and left.

CHAPTER 14

Chu had suggested Shu-chang try speaking to people at the Double Xi and the Phoenix Delight, two wine houses in the vicinity of the burned-out warehouse. As Shu-chang trudged through the streets, trying to keep his long robe free from the dust and filth. He bemoaned the dirt he would have to clean out of his robe's hem later. There was no way to avoid the mess on the street.

The sharp scent of burnt wood still permeated the air. He wondered how long it would be before the town felt clean again. He passed the crime site. Workmen moved like ants through the building's remaining wooden skeleton, removing massive beams and other debris. The Double Xi sat just another block down the road.

Self-conscious as he entered the darkened shop, Shu-chang hoped he looked like he fit in. He'd rarely visited a wine house before today. Nor did his father, who always said he worked for the family's future, not to throw money out the window and into a useless wine house. And he expected the same of his only son.

For as long as Shu-chang remembered, everything had

gone into their bare subsistence and into his education, his chance at bringing honor to the family's name and to their ancestors. Frivolity wasn't tolerated.

He looked around. All of the other men in the room wore traditional laborers' clothing: short jackets and pants tied just below the knee. Some wore stockings, but many simply had bare feet in their rough sandals. They sat clustered around tables sharing drinks. A rumble of conversation moved in waves through the room, rising and falling.

Shu-chang found a small, empty table near the door. Close enough for him to see people and for them to see him, but neither in the center of activity nor hidden away in a corner. He sat and waited. Soon the owner closed in on him, a broad, overly-friendly grin on his face.

"Sir. Welcome to the Double Xi," he said.

Shu-chang cringed. His mourning robe was conspicuous in the wine house. If he could have dressed as a farmer, he wouldn't be noticed. By now, he was so used to wearing the mourning robe, he didn't even think about how it would draw attention. He blew out a puff of air. Too late. He couldn't change in any case. By tradition and law, he was required to wear it for three years to honor his deceased father. He wondered if coming here had been a mistake.

"I would be honored if you'd accept a free jug of wine, good Sir, in honor of your successes," the owner went on.

"Why thank you," Shu-chang said, surprised that his passing the examinations was known in this little shop and relieved that it brought him a level of respect even in the dilapidated tavern. Uncle Xin and Chu had indicated people in the town would be open to him because of his new status, but he had no idea that this would reach down into the lowly taverns. He placed his elbows on the table and leaned forward. This may not be as bad as he thought.

The owner brought a jug of wine and a dish of rice cakes.

He poured wine for Shu-chang and remained standing on the other side of the table, chatting in a loud, familiar manner. As expected, the men at the nearby tables heard every word quite clearly. Finally, a newly arrived group demanded his attention across the room and he went to serve them.

Shu-chang took a rice cake and, feeling more confident, reviewed the men in the room, looking for the most likely candidates for getting information. Should he try to engage the men in the filthy clothing? Could they have been working on cleaning up the burned site? Should he approach the men who wore the stockings and whose clothing, while of the laborer's class, were clean, indicating that they performed no real work? He held the forgotten rice cake up to his lips as he worked out his dilemma.

A burly man, who was not much older than Shu-chang, sidled up to him. "So, you're the important gentleman who is supposed to have given our town a name," he said with a sneer.

The tables around them went quiet.

"And you are?" Shu-chang asked, his eyes dancing around the man to see if he had friends.

"One of the insignificant people who is just waiting to be recognized by such an important man as you."

Shu-chang could see the owner backing up against a wall, an anguished look on his face. Shu-chang felt the same. The few fighting techniques he had learned from his friend Jin-fang had only been used in fun, as a game. In his little village, he never ran into bullies and never had to fight his way out of anything. His stomach tightened and his shoulders tensed. Obviously, this fellow didn't share the owner's feeling about the young scholar.

"Do you have a problem you'd like to discuss?" Shu-chang asked, keeping his voice even.

"Did you think you needed to go among the lowly workers

in order to strut your stuff? Be the big man?" The man had clearly been drinking.

Shu-chang could see that this already unfriendly encounter was going downhill. He forced himself to relax, to be prepared for whatever might come.

"Would you like to sit and have some wine with me?" Shu-chang offered, hoping to derail the man's hostility.

The man scoffed. "I'd rather have wine with my pigs," he said. His voice resonating around the stuffy room. Now the entire tavern had fallen silent.

This was definitely not good.

Out of the corner of his eye, Shu-chang saw the owner finally gather his strength and begin to move in their direction. At the same time, he caught a swift movement—the bully's arm had swung across the table, reaching for Shu-chang's hat. Shu-chang immediately moved to the side, avoiding the grasping hand.

Without meeting resistance, the bully lost his balance and began to fall onto the table. As he fell, he reached out with both hands to seize Shu-chang.

Shu-chang pushed himself back and out of the way. Another of the drunkard's friends came alongside them. He was thin with taut muscles. He reached out for the young scholar, who twisted away and off the stool. Quickly standing, Shu-chang found himself up against a third fellow. He came from the same side as the second attacker.

"Gentlemen. Gentlemen," the owner called out while remaining at a safe distance.

The two new men came at Shu-chang. He gave a side kick to the first man driving him into the third and knocking them both over. By this time, the bully had picked up the table and came at Shu-chang with it. Shu-chang thrust his foot out again, smashing the table in half. The bully stood exposed. He reacted by throwing one of the table pieces aside and grabbing the other by its leg. Rushing at Shu-chang, he brandished the remaining splintered wood like a club. Shu-chang deftly side-stepped the on-coming attack and delivered a sharp kick to the center of the man's chest, sending him sprawling.

Now the three men lay in pain on the dirt-encrusted floor.

Shu-chang shook his head. "You've a lot to learn in fighting, my friends," he said as two sat rubbing their ribs. The third fellow held his head, which he'd hit on a nearby table as his friend had knocked him over.

"Now, wouldn't you rather sit with me and have a cup of wine?" Shu-chang asked.

Bleary eyed, they looked at him as if unable to comprehend his words.

"Join me?" he said again, moving to another empty table, and signaling the owner to bring them wine.

The three stumbled onto their feet, looked around and glared at the men staring at them, and finally sat on the stools around Shu-chang's table. The owner brought wine and more rice cakes and left without saying a word.

Shu-chang poured wine into each of the three men's cups. He poured his own wine and raised his cup to them, giving the familiar drinking toast of "*Gan-bei.*"

The others grinned, took their cups, and drained the wine in one long drink. Shu-chang refilled the cups. He struggled to keep his hand steady and hoped he could keep it up. He was unaccustomed to drinking so much and he'd never been in a brawl, but he didn't want these toughs to think he was a weakling—in anything.

"I'm Zhou," said the bully, "and these are my friends, Lin and Fang."

"You don't sound like you're local," Shu-chang said, noting the accent in their speech.

"We're from a small village outside Fuzhou City in Fujian Province. It's near the sea."

"How did you end up here? You're a long way from Fujian."

"Pirates attacked our village and wiped everyone out. We only escaped because we were working in the forests at the time and not at home. Our families were killed. There was nothing left, so we decided to leave and see what fate had in store for us elsewhere. We came here, to Jian, and found work. So, we stayed."

Shu-chang watched them closely as Zhou spoke. They were simple but strong men.

"And who do you work for?"

"We were working for Gao San-fu until the fire destroyed our jobs," he said, picking up his cup and toasting everyone. They all emptied their cups and reached for a rice cake. Shu-chang drew his cup to his lips and pretended to down the wine in one big gulp, but didn't. When he refilled the men's cups, he passed the jug over his own, as if filling it afresh.

"Ah. And what kind of work did you do for him?"

The three men exchanged glances, then Zhou said, "Whatever he needed done. We weren't particular."

Shu-chang thought he could guess what that work might entail.

"But now that the warehouse has burned down, we might as well move on."

"Doesn't San-fu have other jobs you can do?"

Zhou's eyes briefly flicked towards his friends. "Maybe, but not now, and we have to eat. We can't wait until the warehouse is rebuilt."

"I'm interested in that fire. As you probably know—everyone around here seems to know it—Xiao-ren is being blamed for the crime. For starting the fire and, therefore, accidentally killing two men. Besides being my student, Xiao-ren is a distant cousin on my mother's side, so I've been asked to look into this affair." Shu-chang decided that he might as well be up-front with these men. They undoubtedly already knew more about the incident than he did, and he wanted their trust.

Zhou nodded. "Family," he said. His face seemed to age momentarily as he pressed his hand over his right brow covering his eyes.

Shu-chang did not intrude on his apparently painful memories, instead, he went on: "I wonder if you could tell me what you know about the warehouse incident."

"There's not much to tell. We moved the bags of rice into the secured warehouse as San-fu collected the taxes."

"You put all of the rice into one big room in the warehouse?"

"No. The warehouse was divided into three parts. The bags of rice were in two sections and other items, silk and cotton bolts, special jars of wine, even salt, were kept in the third."

"Hum. I see," Shu-chang said, as he poured more wine for his new informants. Then, on impulse, he suggested, "Why don't you three hang around the town? Something might turn up. San-fu has many businesses that he takes care of. He may need three good men like yourselves."

As the four sat at the table drinking too much and eating several dishes of rich cakes, a tall man in workers' clothing and of impressive demeanor approached. He stopped at their table and introduced himself as Ba-ren.

"So, Xiao-ren is in jail. How unfair! I know him well from the work he's done for San-fu."

Shu-chang was happy to hear someone finally speak so positively about his cousin. "And who are you, sir?"

He nodded in the direction of Shu-chang's three companions and said: "Could we speak in private?"

Zhou pushed back on his stool, rose, and stretched. "Let's go," he said to his friends. "See you again, Sir," he said, nodding toward Shu-chang. The three sauntered over to the far side of the tavern and settled down at another table.

"Good," the newcomer said. He sat down uninvited and folded his hands together on the table. "I'm just another merchant. And, as with almost everyone in the town, I know San-fu and am at least somewhat familiar with what he's doing. In fact, I was there when San-fu hired your cousin, Xiao-ren."

Shu-chang didn't say anything, but he noted that this stranger also knew Xiao-ren was related to him. An extraordinary feat when Shu-chang considered he didn't even know he was related to Xiao-ren before this week when he came to his uncle's home in Jian.

"He's a good lad. I want to help him," the stranger said. "Even if he did this terrible thing, he's so young. He and his family shouldn't be held accountable. I can help.

Shu-chang was so relieved by the man's sympathetic words and to hear that someone else wanted to help Xiao-ren that he eagerly accepted the man's offer.

"Wonderful And how is it you can help Xiao-ren?"

"I have contacts within the court who can assist you."

"How can they do that? Once the magistrate writes up his report, that's it. If the magistrate thinks he did it, and right now he gives every indication he does, Xiao-ren's chances are limited."

The stranger caressed his chin with long thin fingers and bestowed an amused smile on Shu-chang. "It's all quite simple. I have a contact who is able to slightly alter the court depositions and the final verdict with its explanation. My contact has access to all of the court records."

Astonished at this assertion, Shu-chang stared at the stranger. Such a deal sounded like it could solve their problem of finding Xiao-ren guilty as well as the members of his father's extended family. Collective guilt was bedrock in the legal system. But what was the choice? To either abandon Xiao-ren to be tortured in jail until the upper courts determine his fate or rescue the young man by breaking the law themselves? The family had already paid an extraordinary amount for Xiao-ren's safety while he waited to be called into court in the next day or two. This plan would require even more resources, more money. Plus, it was illegal and came with its own set of risks to the Xin clan.

CHAPTER 15

Xiang-hua replaced the blanket on the elder woman, one of the oldest members of the Xin family. She stepped away from the wooden kang and followed the woman's daughter-in-law into the main room of the house. As they entered, the woman's son, Kan, invited her to sit near him in one of the simple wooden chairs arranged along the wall before the family's ancestral altar. His wife took the chair on his other side.

"How is she doing?" he asked in a low voice.

"Not well." This was one of the parts of being a doctor that Xiang-hua hated: having to tell family that their loved one couldn't be helped.

The daughter-in-law nodded. "As I told you when you arrived, she's been in a lot of pain lately." She glanced at her husband and he nodded in agreement.

"I'll give you medicine to keep her comfortable." Xiang-hua tried to offer the sympathy her grandmother did at such times. "Your mother is seventy-seven years old and has been a virtuous example for all of us. It is getting close to the time for her to join her husband and your ancestors. You should prepare for it."

"How much time do we have?" her son asked.

"Perhaps a week, maybe a month."

The couple accepted the news with calm, but Xiang-hua suspected that once alone they would allow themselves to express their grief.

"Father! Father!" called out a strong male voice. Like a wind blowing into the room, a man in his early thirties strode through the doorway. Seeing Xiang-hua and his parents sitting huddled together, he abruptly stopped.

"Please excuse me," he said offering a slight bow.

"Sister Xin, this is our son, Huei," his father said. "Son, Sister has come to attend to your grandmother. Do you have a reason to bother us at this time?"

The younger man bowed lower to Xiang-hua, who nodded at his courtesy. Then he addressed his father: "I'm sorry to interrupt, but I have something important I must tell you." He seemed to be bursting with news.

As if an even heavier weight had just been placed on him, his father's shoulders slumped. He rose and the two men stepped outside of the room.

The younger man was barely out of the room when Xiang-hua heard him say, "There's nothing I could do. San-fu refused to see me."

His mother turned to Xiang-hua. "I'm sorry for my son's interruption, Sister, but I fear that at this critical time of my mother-in-law's dying, my husband also has problems with the land." She looked at the ancestral altar and the tablet with her father-in-law's name inscribed on it.

Xiang-hua suspected that, as with many families she visited, Xin's problems were the result of the exorbitant fees San-fu now charged farmers to cultivate their own lands. She looked around the room. Scrolls hung from its walls, each with an admonition for families to live in harmony and protect the family line. This was a good, middle-class home: not wealthy, but not poor either. It seemed San-fu's new policies were destroying everyone.

"San-fu," Xiang-hua said.

"Ah, so you know." The woman almost smiled as she looked at Xiang-hua. "Of course, you would know." She shifted in her chair, turning her body toward Xiang-hua even as her attention remained glued to the door her husband and son had exited through.

"How are other families dealing with this?" she asked.

Xiang-hua lifted her hand in a movement of frustration. "Some, who couldn't pay the higher fee, have been turned out of their homes and are struggling to make a living in the town as laborers wherever they can. The few who can pay are worried about next year. What if the crops don't do any better than in the past? They, too, may lose the right to work their own ancestral lands."

The woman faced Xiang-hua. "My son is livid over this. We have never had a problem in all these years. The fee Master Gao demanded was fair and the crops were good—until recently. I don't understand why Master Gao is doing this. It may be legal, but it wasn't the implicit agreement he had with all of the landowners whose land he placed under his umbrella."

"It looks like he is distributing the lands to other members of his own clan. As far as I can tell, all of the lands and houses he's confiscated were from Xin clan members," Xiang-hua said.

"That would explain why my son has been raving about the Gao clan having a stranglehold on the Xin clan."

"I can understand why he'd be so upset."

"Yes, but I'm worried about him. He works himself into a frenzy every night over this. I know it's serious, perhaps even critical to our survival as a family. But I'm worried he might do something dangerous. Something that will bring greater calamity on our house." She stared at Xiang-hua as if seeing through her. "Perhaps he already has."

Lost in thought, Xiang-hua strode through the streets as she returned home. So many families were losing the rights to their own lands because of what their fathers and grandfathers had done years ago. Could any one of them, or perhaps even a group of them, have burned down the warehouse to teach the Gao family a lesson? There was enough anger brewing in the town and the surrounding villages for it to have come to a boil and culminate in such an action. If that were the case, would they let one of their own clan members, Xiao-ren, take the blame? She shook her head. No, that didn't make sense. They'd try to blame a Gao for sure. Unless, of course, a Xin also had a grudge against Xiao-ren.

She frowned. Her little brother was always into something he shouldn't be. She could see him offending someone and thinking nothing of it. For the offended person, an attack against the Gao family while laying the blame on Xiao-ren—could prove to be the perfect revenge.

Rounding a corner, Xiang-hua almost ran into Shu-chang.

"Xiang-hua, it's good to see you. I should have known you would be out working."

She smiled up at him. "And what are you doing out of the classroom, Teacher?"

"Trying to catch the early crowd in the wine house. They are probably different than the ones I met last night."

The smile died on her face. "I hope you find something we can take to the court. I seem to be getting possibilities, but nothing concrete." She repeated what she had learned on her visit to Xin Kan's home. How angry his son Huei was with San-fu. Huei's mother's concerns.

Shu-chang stood close to her, listening intently.

"Ah, two of my favorite people."

Xiang-hua and Shu-chang turned as one and faced Granny. Although she was only an arm's length away, neither had noticed her. Xiang-hua felt her face grow hot.

"Let's move out of the main crush of the traffic," Granny suggested, ignoring her discomfort.

They moved against a wall and formed a tight circle, with Xiang-hua carefully managing to stand closer to Granny than Shu-chang.

"I was just coming to see you, Teacher. The silk merchant was able to tell me many interesting things." She smacked her lips as if eating a delicious meal.

"And this is not rumor. This is what he knows—or claims he knows—for sure."

"Good. Because up to this point, we've only been getting rumors, nothing more," Shu-chang said.

"That warehouse was used to hide illegal goods. Since it is the official building designated to hold the Emperor's rice as payment for taxes, it's never inspected for contraband as the other warehouses are."

"Contraband? What are you talking about?" Shu-chang asked.

"Do you mean someone was selling to the barbarians without a government license?" Xiang-hua asked.

Granny grinned. "It's just as you say. Those western barbarians want to trade with us, but the Emperor isn't interested."

Shu-chang nodded. "Well, they forcefully stole our country and established their own dynasty, the Yuan Dynasty. The Chinese were ruled by foreigners for several generations. It hasn't been that long since our esteemed Emperor Hongwu finally won it back. Not too many Han Chinese want to trade with them."

"But some do," Granny pointed out.

"Money; it always comes down to money," Xiang-hua said. "Because the foreigners want to trade more than we do, they will pay exorbitant amounts for our goods."

"That's exactly what's happening," Granny said. "A small network of merchants are selling goods on the black market to the barbarians and making a great profit."

"Was your merchant friend able to give you a name?" Xiang-hua asked.

Granny fairly danced. "Gao San-fu, Master Gao's grandson."

Xiang-hua eyes opened wide in surprise. Shu-chang clapped his hands as if bringing a closing to an argument. Granny looked back and forth between them, her body bouncing with excitement.

"Yes, San-fu is definitely the leader. It makes sense. Through his grandfather's position and status, he has control of most of the town—including the security teams," Shu-chang said.

"Most importantly, he collects the taxes. The illegal goods traded to the barbarians come from the government itself. The merchant claims San-fu collects a higher percentage of tax than needed and reports less on the official ledger. He blames the weather and poor crops for any shortfall." Granny clicked her tongue to show disagreement with such a scheme.

"And all government correspondence goes first through his grandfather and, therefore, him. Once his grandfather's seal is on the report, it passes through the people San-fu's placed in the yamen," Xiang-hua said. "So, no one in the government knows the difference."

Granny nodded and grinned. "Clever."

"But how does that fit into burning down the warehouse?"

Shu-chang asked. "He wouldn't destroy his own business, would he?"

Granny nodded. It didn't make sense.

"Look underneath the surface. The problem was that when the new inspector, who was definitely coming, found a disparity between the tax records and the amount actually collected—that is, what was stored in the warehouse—there would be an investigation. Undoubtedly, San-fu would be found guilty. He would be executed. Cheating on taxes is the same as treason. His Majesty's punishment would be severe," Xiang-hua said.

The old woman wrinkled her brow and shook her head in agreement.

"So, you are saying he started the fire and blamed your brother," Shu-chang said staring at Xiang-hua.

Granny crackled with glee. "It has to be him. Now we can get Xiao-ren released from prison."

"If we can prove it," Xiang-hua said. "Shu-chang, it looks like you need to make another trip to the local wine shops."

CHAPTER 16

This time when Shu-chang strode into the Double Xi, he was greeted warmly by the owner and a few of the men scattered around the tables. He made a mental note to learn everyone's name this time, especially the names of those men who were here in the evening and could still be found in the tavern during the day. They would be well poised to observe what was happening in the street and privy to the area's goings-on.

He was surprised to see his three new friends lounging around a table in the back. He went to join them.

"If it isn't our scholar," Zhou said genially. "If you keep this up, you'll be like the rest of us: jobless." His wide grin revealed missing teeth. Lin and Fang smiled at Zhou's humor and leaned forward on their arms as if ready to listen to news.

Shu-chang chuckled and pulled up a stool.

"If I had any money, I'd hire you guys. You would make great look-outs."

At this attempt at levity, Shu-chang noticed a quick sharing of concerned glances pass around the three. Had he hit onto something? He followed that up with what he hoped was a significant look at each of them. "Perhaps you have had experience in that field already."

Zhou's laugh this time sounded somewhat strained. "What would make you think that? We're just simple laborers looking for jobs."

"Hey, what're you guys doing with that ne'er-do-well?"

Zhou, Lin, and Fang's faces all went blank, showing no emotion. "Good to see you, San-fu," Zhou called out to a well-dressed, thickset fellow.

"Come join us," San-fu called over as he chose a table near the door for himself and the three men with him.

Shu-chang rose with his companions. "Not you, Teacher," San-fu said firmly. "Just my men."

Shu-chang sunk back onto his stool as Zhou and the others quickly left the table.

Without being waved over, the owner was already bringing wine and onion cakes for their table. He poured for all the men and left.

Shu-chang had expected the table to be loud and raucous, but, instead, their conversation was low and muted. He couldn't hear a word and there was no way he could move over to their table. There wasn't even anyone close to them that he knew and could question discreetly later.

He looked around the room. Now everyone avoided his eyes; most men looked away or suddenly appeared to be in deep conversation with their mates. Obviously, once San-fu came into the tavern, Shu-chang became *persona non-grata*.

Interesting, Shu-chang thought. Did San-fu consider him, and his inquires about who was responsible for the fire and the deaths, a threat? He reasoned that anyone would be unhappy if they thought a stranger was trying to tie them to serious crimes, so San-fu's reactions may not be an admission of guilt. On the other hand, he was head of almost everything around here and should be accustomed to people inquiring about him and his activities.

Shu-chang cast a covert glance at Zhou and his friends sitting at San-fu's table. They were bent toward San-fu and listening carefully.

Shu-chang lifted his cup and took a sip. So, were they really out of a job, or was that just a ruse to be able to sit around in taverns in order to learn more about the rumor mill?

As Shu-chang was turning these thoughts over, a gangly man wearing the robes of a court runner entered the tavern. He stopped at the entrance and scanned the room. Seeing Shu-chang, he came over to his table.

"Sir, may I join you?" His formal request in such a place struck Shu-chang as remarkably out of place.

"Of course, please sit." As the man folded himself onto the stool, Shu-chang said, "I'm sorry, I'm at a disadvantage here. Who are you?"

"My name is Xin Guei-hu. I'm a runner for the court, so of course I know all about you and your great accomplishments." He said while waving for the owner to come to their table. "A cup for me and another jug of wine with whatever snack you have." He turned toward Shu-chang. "I hope you don't mind my ordering for both of us?"

"Thank you for your generosity," Shu-chang said. He was delighted to have a staff member of the court join him, but also confused as to why this fellow sought him out. Given the complexities of the moment, was this really a coincidence? He'd have to let this fellow play out his gambit, whatever it was. Shu-chang could analyze the situation later.

"I understand you are interested in the burning of the warehouse and the deaths of those two men," the runner began unceremoniously.

Shu-chang nodded.

"I am coming to you as a representative of the magistrate. He wishes to keep abreast of all that is going on. He fully realizes that it is more difficult for his own investigators to get at the truth—people often lie to them—than for an outsider who can dig deeper." He dropped his quiet voice even more. "It would be beneficial to the court if you shared whatever you discovered as you went along. Do you understand?"

"Completely. You are representing His Honor, the magistrate." Shu-chang repeated what he'd just been told.

The runner allowed a quick nod. "For the sake of security, we could meet here, rather than you having to go into the court to report your findings."

Shu-chang nodded again. What else could he do? There was no refusing the court. And yet, he knew that the court was infiltrated with staff who could change the flow of events. Making the innocent appear guilty and the guilty appear innocent. This would require his highest level of diplomacy—a skill which, up until now, he was most aware that he had never needed nor honed.

"Good. I have permission to tell you a few things about His Honor's investigations up to this point."

Shu-chang was delighted, but kept his face as neutral as possible.

"The fire occurred the day before His Honor's men were to inspect the warehouse for stolen goods. The fact that the fire, which destroyed all evidence, happened mysteriously the day before raised questions in his mind. He suspects purposeful arson to hide evidence, which would have brought down a powerful network of illegal trading." The runner watched Shu-chang carefully. "So, you can imagine how important it is to him to find the perpetrators and why he wants your help."

There was no way that Shu-chang could refuse. He pursed his lips and nodded in reply.

"Good." The man rose. "I will return to the court and inform His Honor of your decision to assist him."

As the man left the tavern, Shu-chang looked over at San-fu's table. It was now empty as well. All of his gang, including Zhou, Lin, and Fang, had left.

Shu-chang lifted his cup and wondered what he had gotten into. The wine burned his throat and stomach. He put the empty cup down, crossed his arms on the table, and gently placed his head on them. He felt a bit queasy; he wasn't used to drinking so much, and needed a short rest. The tavern's noise muted into nothing.

Soon Shu-chang found himself sitting amongst his friends, drinking and dining. They commiserated about how difficult the Provincial examination was and how thankful they were that they'd at least survived the ordeal.

Time flowed by. He lost track of how long they'd shared drinking games while dainty dishes of luscious foods were brought by the host's lovely maids. He lost more games than he won, so that his face had become a bright red and his eyes lost focus. The world around him teetered. He giggled at his friends' mundane comments and poorly executed poetry.

Reaching for another cup of wine, he miscalculated, and it tipped over. Wine covered the table and dribbled onto his white robe. A maid sopped the mess up while he profusely apologized to those around him. Their laughter filled his ears and their open mouth guffaws dominated his vision until he could see nothing else. His senses were overwhelmed by the noise and sights around him. He closed his eyes and held his head. It didn't help. He only felt dizzier with the world moving even more uncontrollably.

He pushed away from the table and struggled to stand. "I must be getting home," he said, his voice slurred.

With an unsteady gait, he made it to the street. It was late and there were few people about. No one paid him any attention as he stumbled down the hard-packed road. He walked near the buildings' walls so that he could stop periodically and touch one to stabilize himself on his journey.

It was at one such stop that he noticed two men approaching him. They both limped badly and clung to each other for support as they walked. Their clothing was torn, dirty, and covered in blood. Shu-chang wanted to look away, but couldn't.

As they came closer he saw their faces. It was his father and uncle. Their eyes were hollow; their skin a ghastly grey. Blood dripped from the top of their heads into their eyes and down their cheeks. Shu-chang stood rigid, rooted in place.

He wanted to run to them. To help them. To embrace them. And--at the same time--he wanted to run away from them and their terrifying visages. It was too much. He slumped against the wall, his head swimming.

"Shu-chang." It sounded a little like his father, but the tone was low and almost a moan.

The hair stood up on the back of Shu-chang's head. "*Fu-chin*?" he said, turning toward the speaker.

"Don't you know me?"

Shu-chang fell onto his knees and kowtowed.

"Why are you drinking and carousing when our killers are running free? What kind of son are you? Don't you have any respect for all we've done for you? Is this how you repay your family?"

Shu-chang shrank away. Guilt replaced fear. He was unfilial, unworthy as a son.

"We cannot rest in peace until we have justice."

Shu-chang kowtowed several times to his father. "I will find them. I promise. One way or another, there will be justice for you and for uncle," he said into the ground, not daring to face his father with his failure.

He waited for his father's response.

All was quiet.

Shu-chang waited. His sweat trickled onto the ground, forming a ghostly puddle. He couldn't raise his head. Was his father so angry that he wouldn't, or couldn't, speak?

The silence only increased his misery. He should have done more. How could he even think of anything else? This task must come first.

He waited.

Nothing but a general mumble of unclear voices washed over him.

Finally, shaking his head, Shu-chang opened his eyes. Finding himself slumped over a roughly marred table, he unsteadily looked around. The street scene with his father and uncle was gone, replaced by the Double Xi tavern's dingy interior and its scruffy patrons. He rose and, with his hand against the building's wall for support, he carefully examined the room around him. His father and uncle had disappeared.

But he knew they were not gone. Their spirits roamed because they died before their time and without justice.

He missed them, missed seeing them, missed working and laughing with them. But missing them was not enough. He had a duty to his father and uncle that must be fulfilled. Even as he worked on the Xin case, he could not forget them and their need for justice. It was his destiny.

CHAPTER 17

With his heart still racing, Shu-chang noted that little had changed in his surroundings since he closed his eyes. Even the same men were drinking and playing dice games around him, suggesting he couldn't have been asleep for more than a few minutes. Finally pulling himself together, he ordered tea and remained at the Double Xi until dark. He had an obligation to the Xin family to help and he would keep that commitment.

While he had met several of the men who worked off and on in the area, none provided any useful information. Finally, he started on his way back to Uncle Xin's house. He had barely left the wine house when a short, muscular man in his fifties came up from behind. He slowed down and matched Shu-chang's stride, staying parallel with him.

Shu-chang gave a side-ways glance at the fellow, taking in his heavily dirt-encrusted, short jacket and pants, which were tied just below his knee. The man ignored his gaze and continued to nonchalantly walk alongside, as if keeping pace was an accident.

"Greetings, Sir," Shu-chang said.

"And to you," the man replied. He looked away, then back. "I hear you're interested in the warehouse fire."

"You've heard correctly," Shu-chang said, curious as to what this fellow had to say.

"I'm Chen and I've been working for Master Gao since I was a boy. A couple of years ago his grandson, San-fu, took over the different branches of the family business. Now I work for him."

Shu-chang's heart raced. Was this man about to bring him insider information or was he here to warn Shu-chang off of his investigation? He waited.

"In his warehouses," Chen said, as if clarifying, to be sure Shu-chang understood the connection between his workplace and what he was about to say. "He has three: the one for the Emperor's taxes, one for his own storage, and a third warehouse that he rents to merchants from other regions."

Shu-chang took the phrase "merchants from other regions" to mean other ethnic groups, non-Han traders. They had to store their merchandise someplace when they came. Renting space in the Gao warehouse was good business. The location was convenient to an important main street and its shops. Plus, doing business with Gao gave them an informal tie to the most influential family in the area. Nothing wrong with that. Just normal business practice.

"Which one did you work in this past week?"

The man smiled grimly, took a deep breath, then said, "The one that was destroyed."

Shu-chang cast a long look at the man trudging along beside him. "You're lucky you weren't working the night the warehouse burned or you might be another body in the rubble."

The man winced.

A thought hit Shu-chang. He stopped mid-step and stared

at the stranger. "You worked at the warehouse, so you knew the men who were killed."

Chen scanned the people around them, as if checking the crowd for an unwelcome guest. "I did. I knew them." He didn't sound happy. "Could we continue walking?"

Shu-chang scrutinized the neighborhood himself, saw nothing special, but proceeded ahead all the same. Whatever made the stranger comfortable enough to tell him more.

"The guards were simply poor souls who worked for San-fu—which really everyone should know. It was their bad fate to be working that night."

"And you don't know anything more about them. Anything that would have made their deaths purposeful and not just an accident? Did they do any other work besides guarding the building, for example?" Shu-chang asked. He didn't think the stranger would be able to say more, but he wanted to cover all possible avenues in his investigation.

Chen clenched his hands into fists. "Might be." He opened and closed his hands as he moved along beside Shu-chang, not looking at him, just talking while vigilantly perusing the people in the street around them. "All of San-fu's workers do whatever he requires. That's our job."

Shu-chang nodded and again glanced at the muscled form. He appeared to be more thug than laborer. Farmers were strong—they had to be for the hard work in the fields—but not muscled the way this fellow was. He was built more like a fighter.

Shu-chang thought back to his fight with Zhou, Lin, and Fang in the bar. They fought like amateurs. They'd never trained in martial arts. Assessing the man beside him, Shu-chang hoped he'd never have to use his own limited skills against him. He was lucky the first time and he didn't want to test his luck again.

"Well, what I heard is that you wanted to know who was

hanging around the warehouse that night. Is that right or not?" Chen said with a cord of belligerence running through the question.

"I'd like to hear whatever you can tell me," Shu-chang said. He didn't fail to register that Chen had quickly changed the topic from the two guards.

"Right then. As I said, I was there that night, but I had gone outside to take a break. I was sitting on a bench eating a dumpling when I saw Huei. You probably know him. He's Kan's son. I noticed him because he's been hanging around trying to see San-fu. He's got quite a temper."

"Did you talk to him?"

"Na. What about? I don't need more trouble and that's what he is: trouble."

"Have you told the magistrate any of this?" Shu-chang asked.

"No one asked me anything and I'm not going to volunteer. You know it's better to stay away from the law. But," he stared meaningfully at Shu-chang, "if the judge's soldiers come and ask me, I'll tell them what I know. I'm not going to lie to the court."

A heavy weight dropped onto Shu-chang. Xin Kan and his son Huei were his mother's cousins. His feet began to drag. A tightness in his chest made it difficult for him to breathe.

This fellow could be lying, however, Shu-chang had already heard from Xiang-hua about his temper and hatred toward the Gao family for what San-fu was doing. It grieved him to say it, but Shu-chang believed this fellow.

The magistrate wanted to know everything he found out in his investigations. His eyes slid toward the stranger again. There was no way he was going to report this. Loyalty to his extended family over-shadowed any agreement with the magistrate.

His head began to throb as he now wondered if by investigating the destruction of the building in order to free Xiao-ren, he would instead ensnare his mother's cousin's and his uncle's fellow clan member. He morosely thought about how much less complex life had been just a few short weeks ago, when he was a simple student studying for exams.

They walked in silence towards a larger intersection. As they reached it, Chen turned toward Shu-chang. "I wanted you to know. I won't say anything—unless the judge brings me into court." With that he veered off onto the crossroad and disappeared into the crowd.

Shu-chang meandered on. The man might actually do what he says and keep silent. The problem, as Shu-chang saw it, was that he was sure it was just a matter of time before the court found out about Chen being at the site the night of the arson. That is, if the court hadn't already settled on Xiao-ren as the culprit.

Shu-chang rubbed his temple. In either scenario, the Xin clan was in trouble. All signs pointed to one member or another of their clan. He pressed his lips into a tight line as the words *serious trouble, serious trouble* tumbled around in his head.

Lost in thought, Shu-chang no longer paid attention to his surroundings. The business section fell away and the crowd thinned out to nothing, leaving him sauntering alone through darkened streets. Distracted, caught up in his own musings, he never heard a door open or the flurry of footfalls until it was too late.

The first punch to his stomach seemed to come out of nowhere. Shu-chang gasped and bent over in pain. Stumbling away from the impact, he crashed against the cold, hard surface of a nearby wall. With his pulse racing, he forced his way through shock and fear. Then, using the wall as a catalyst, he thrust a leg out, aimed at the attacker. His instincts for full battle mode completely engaged. He felt a jolt run up his calf and thigh as he struck his target.

"Oomph!" The attacker stumbled to the side and recovered.

At the same time, Shu-chang fell back, almost tripping. He regained his footing, but his leg muscles started trembling uncontrollably. Focusing, he rose up on the balls of his feet, then firmly set his heels on the road, regaining a neutral, ready stance.

As the attacker again moved to strike Shu-chang, a second man circled behind and went for a punch. Catching the movement at his back, Shu-chang immediately stabbed a foot up and back. Another jolt through his leg told him he'd made contact.

"Aie!" The second assailant called out, as he crumbled into the dirt.

In the meantime, the first man again attacked. Shu-chang hadn't regained his footing after the back leg thrust, and he couldn't respond fast enough. He stumbled under the brigand's blow, but managed to avoid falling.

He looked ahead. Uncle Xin's entrance wasn't far away. He only needed to make it to the gate, then he'd be safe. He determined to double his efforts—if that were possible —and spun about to elude his attackers and give himself time to renew his fighting stance while moving closer to the gate.

His attackers joined together to strike simultaneously from two sides. Shu-chang jumped and spun, arms and legs flying out, ready to strike whoever was in range. His right leg, then the left, each made contact. He stumbled back into position.

A quick glance showed his adversaries down, but not out. His eyes darted toward Uncle Xin's gate.

"Get him!" One of the thugs yelled to his companion, as he struggled to stand up.

Shu-chang didn't need any more notice, he whirled around and dashed through the gate and into safety.

Once inside, he collapsed onto his knees, gulping for air. His abrupt and explosive entrance set Uncle Xin's chickens into an extreme state of excitement. Their terrified clucking and frantic flights through open doors and windows along the surrounding veranda drew the family out into the small courtyard.

Before he knew it, Uncle Xin was helping him stand and walk into his room, while he heard his Aunt Nu-er's high pitched voice call out that she was going to prepare hot water and bring clean cloths.

That's the last Shu-chang heard before he passed out. When he woke up he was in his own bed.

"What happened out there?" his uncle demanded. "I would expect this from Xiao-ren, but never from you." His tone was accusatory and, at the same time, filled with disappointment.

Shu-chang closed his eyes. He didn't need this. Did his uncle seriously think he'd just gotten into a random fight, perhaps from drinking too much? Well, he'd explain, but right now he hurt too much. He had no energy. He kept his eyes closed and soon fell asleep.

When he woke up, he saw Uncle Xin sitting in the same position he'd been in earlier. Shu-chang raised himself up on his elbow.

"It's about time you woke up," his uncle said. He smiled but it didn't hide the worry and disappointment in his eyes. "Are you ready to tell me what happened?"

"I was returning to the house when two thugs attacked me. Fortunately, we weren't too far from your gate. But not close enough," he added ruefully.

"Any idea who they were? Had you seen them before? Perhaps at the Double Xi?"

"I don't think they were at the Double Xi. They could have been robbers. It was late and dark and I was alone."

"Possible, but by now most people know you're a teacher. What would they expect to steal from you?"

His uncle's assumption that an itinerant scholar must be penniless hit a nerve. Such a life of poverty was the very thing Shu-chang's father wanted him to escape and why he had worked so hard to pay for his son's education. It was supposed to be Shu-chang's chance for a better life.

Shu-chang took a deep breath before replying. "Hum. I was returning from the Double Xi, as you say. Maybe the attack was a warning to stop my investigation of the fire and deaths."

"Did either of the men threaten you? Demand you quit?"

Shu-chang shook his head and immediately wished he hadn't; the motion caused his headache to reach nauseating proportions.

"So that doesn't seem right, either," his uncle said.

Irritated that his every suggestion was dismissed, Shu-chang said, "What else could it be?"

"The attack was too clumsy, too poorly executed. Old man Gao would never use such methods. He was always more sophisticated in his strong-arm techniques."

"Strong-arm techniques? Master Gao?" Shu-chang said incredulously. He had a hard time imagining an old man using such methods.

"He's old now, but he wasn't always old. And, scholar or not, he could be ruthless in the pursuit of what he wanted. Every man is capable of great cruelty if they are thwarted in achieving their goals. Don't forget that." He gazed out the window as if looking into the past. "No, Master Gao would have used more indirect and discreet means."

In spite of what his uncle claimed, Shu-chang was convinced the attack was a warning. But by whom and for what? What was he missing?

CHAPTER 18

The next morning, the boys stood tall and straight as Shu-chang entered the room. They called out "Good Morning, Teacher" in loud, clear voices.

He stared at his little crop of students with their unruly hair sticking out at odd angles and their clothing almost, but not quite, right for young scholars. Their pants and jackets were well-worn and, despite many washings—or perhaps because of too many washings—did not appear crisp and clean. They looked like what they were: poor town and village youngsters.

But today they stood bright and attentive, ready to learn. He touched the large bruise on his left cheek. Undoubtedly, they had heard about the street fight he had been in the night before.

"Sit and open your books," he said.

They readily obeyed. There would be no impish comments and misbehavior today. Shu-chang hid the smile tugging at his lips by busying himself with getting his own materials ready. Being in a street brawl wasn't the reason students should behave, but it worked for today.

With his face again settled into a neutral pose, he turned back to the boys and the day began.

At mid-day, the students went home to complete their memorizations. Shu-chang hastened to put his things in order and abandoned the room. He quickened his pace as he moved down the road towards town. He didn't want to waste daylight. This was a good time for him to personally examine the site of the fire.

Coming up on the warehouse's remains, he slowed down. The smell of wet ash permeated the area. Standing off to one side, there was still a small group of curious on-lookers pausing as they went about their various marketing tasks of buying or selling. A myriad of men crawled over the burnt-out structure's carcass. Several workers removed partially destroyed timbers; others scooped up smaller debris and hauled it off on wheel barrows. A block away, at the other end of the structure, Shu-chang saw a tall man calling out orders as he stepped through the ruble. San-fu.

Shu-chang grimaced. He didn't want a run-in with Master Gao's grandson. He carefully inspected the crew nearest to him. He spied Zhou and his two friends at work. They had just filled a cart and Zhou began dragging it away. Shu-chang followed.

A large wagon stood beyond the main structure and behind a small shed, which had miraculously escaped the fire. Zhou emptied his cart into the wagon.

"Good to see you, Zhou," Shu-chang said.

Zhou looked up, his face streaked with sweat and dirt. "Well, if it isn't the Teacher. Skipping school again?" He grinned.

"You look like you could use a break."

Zhou shook his head. "Not if I want to keep my job."

"So, you've found work again. Does that mean you're going to stay in town a while?"

"Might as well. One place is as good as another."

Behind the casual comment, Shu-chang wondered if he heard the whisper of a lost soul. He and his friends were far from their homes, with little possibility of going back. Such a thing meant they were rootless. Being rootless meant they had the freedom to go anywhere; it also meant they had no family, no community, no place in the world.

Shu-chang nodded toward the debris. "This is a massive project. It should take a while."

"The boss wants it cleaned up posthaste so the warehouse can be rebuilt. It has to be ready for the rest of this year's taxes." He leaned against the cart and wiped his face with his sleeve. Rivulets of dirt and grime became swirls of grey and black. "What are you doing here? Still investigating?" He squinted at Shu-chang's cheekbone. "I heard you had a rough night."

"I ran into a couple of cranky guys on the way home."

"They gave you a nice present." He touched his own cheek and gave him a commiserating grin.

Shu-chang ran his fingers over his bruise. "We did some sparring."

"Are scholars supposed to be out brawling? You're going to have to give it up," Zhou said with a much wider smile.

Shu-chang laughed, then changed the subject. "Have you heard anything new?"

"Nothing."

"I'd appreciate it if you'd keep an eye open." He was reaching when he suggested that Zhou gather information for him, but he needed an inside man and—as an outsider himself—he had none other than his only recently re-established ties to his mother's extended family. A fact he was perpetually aware of. At least there was a possibility that Zhou could assist. This was no time to be timid.

To his relief, Zhou nodded his head without comment. He looked around before adding: "Well, I've got to get back. The boss will notice I'm gone." And with that, Zhou left.

Shu-chang looked after the burly man's retreating figure and hoped he would really keep watch for him. He returned to the street, walking along the back of the site. Among the fallen sections of wall and roof, he recognized mounds of goods. *Probably some of the piles of the stored rice which hadn't burned but were still ruined*, he thought. *The Emperor will not be happy to learn that his taxes were destroyed.*

"Hey, you there! What're you doing?"

Shu-chang--pulled out of his reflections—looked up. San-fu stood on a pile of rubble, glaring down at him. This was just what he wanted to avoid. Now he must try to make the best of the situation.

"Afternoon, San-fu," Shu-chang greeted the angry visage in what he hoped sounded like a friendly voice.

"This is private property," San-fu said.

Shu-chang nodded amicably. "And I'm in the public alley-way, just observing like the rest of the good citizens." He waved his hand toward the upper street with its gawkers still clustered around and watching the workers.

San-fu smirked. "I heard you had a run-in last night. You'd better be careful or the magistrate won't honor your passing the examinations at all. Instead you'll be listed with your criminal cousins."

San-fu's dig touched a sore spot with Shu-chang. It was all he could do to not respond with anger or hostility. On the other hand, he was all-too aware of the real possibility that either Xiao-ren or another of the Xin clan would be found guilty of arson and accidental murder.

Before San-fu could continue his bullying, a young man

ran up to them. "Boss, we need you over on the south corner."

San-fu cursed and spat toward Shu-chang, then turned on his heel and left without another word.

Shu-chang continued along the road, searching the debris as much as he could from such a distance, but to no avail. Finally, he gave up and went home, admitting as he did so that he didn't know what he hoped to find anyhow. A written document saying who started the fire and why? Ah, not likely. He glumly pulled at his robe and strode home.

That evening after supper, Shu-chang and Xiang-hua sat across from each other at a table in the classroom. A long sheet of rice paper had been spread out; inkstone and ink were ready. Shu-chang wanted to see her calligraphy. It would tell him a lot about his student. How one wrote was as important as what one wrote. Style reflected personality and moral strength. Such was its level of importance that it was considered a critical part in passing the government examinations. He had worked diligently to develop a strong, firm style.

Xiang-hua carefully and deliberately filled the tip of her brush with ink. She was not rushed, nor did she appear intimidated by her new teacher. Once satisfied with how full her brush was, she held the tip in the air over the paper, studying the sheet as it lay in front of her. Then, with swift, yet unhurried, stokes, she let her brush fly. He watched her strong, sure hand as the beautiful characters spread across the page.

He sat back in wonder. This young woman was a constant surprise. He'd expected a more delicate, feminine style, not this.

As she concentrated, he observed her as if for the first time. He still didn't believe she was particularly beautiful, yet he couldn't help but be attracted to her. He watched her as she was completely engrossed in her writing. He noted the crease between her eyes and her puckered lips.

She finished, paused a moment, and looked up at him. He hurriedly glanced away, then down at the paper.

"Not bad."

He caught her momentary pout at his assessment, but didn't change his short comment.

They worked along for a while, with him giving instructions and her complying. He found himself wishing any one of his boys would do as well. Then he'd be happy.

As she worked, he leaned against the chair's back and crossed his arms. He sighed.

"What's the matter?" she demanded.

Startled, Shu-chang sat up. This girl! Yes, she's a doctor, but she's also his student. Such directness was completely out of the question.

"You look troubled," she said, laying her brush down on the inkstone. She placed the palms of her hands together, pressed the fingers on either hand against each other, and pushed, driving the tension out of her right hand.

He nodded and, closing his eyes, pinched the bridge of his nose. She was right, after all. "There are too many people. And all the wrong people—Xin clan members," he clarified as he gazed at her, "—who could have committed these crimes.

"I was down at the warehouse today. There's no new information, so right now that leaves your brother and possibly Xin Kan's son Huei as prime suspects. They seem to be the most logical perpetrators. They're both hot-blooded, and anger could lead to hatred. Revenge would be a strong motive to destroy the warehouse with the rice in it. San-fu was responsible for collecting and keeping the Emperor's taxes safe. With this disaster, he could be accused of not carrying out his duties to the Emperor and, therefore, in serious trouble. It's possible San-fu and his family could lose everything."

"Meaning that burning the warehouse would not help him, only make trouble for him," Xiang-hua said.

"Right," Shu-chang agreed. "Several people claim to have seen your brother or other Xin men in the vicinity of the building before the fire. There's no one else who's even been mentioned who didn't belong there. We don't seem to be getting anywhere. Unless, of course, we define progress as our discovering guilty scenarios for young men in the Xin family." He frowned.

Xiang-hua leaned forward. "Hatred is one thing, but is it enough for such an extreme action? One that is against His Majesty, as well as against San-fu?"

He had expected an emotional diatribe against San-fu, but her thinking was rational. Her cool head was all the more impressive given that her family's lives—including her own—were at stake. "What else could it be? Right now, it is the best motive we have."

She shook her head. "Perhaps we are looking in the wrong direction. Who gains the most from the fire? I know it's hard to imagine, but someone has to have gotten something of importance out of this. Vengeance? Perhaps, but we must look beyond that. Maybe the fire has to do with the dead men and not the loss of goods. They still haven't been identified."

He studied her face. This odd young woman may have opened another avenue for them to investigate. After a lengthy discussion of everyone they knew who was involved and of every possible motive they could think of, they came to only one conclusion: they had no solid answers, but they couldn't give up. They'd each continue gathering whatever information they could. However, since Xiang-hua had to prepare medicine before attending to Erh-xi-fu, they decided that Shu-chang should go alone to talk with Granny, to convince her to join them in discovering what had really happened and who was involved.

———

It didn't take Shu-chang long to find Granny. Everyone knew her and knew where she was as she moved through the town in her mysterious missions. He waited for her to come out of a silk merchant's shop.

"Teacher," she said on spying him on the street. "How good to see you."

"I've come to ask if you wanted to stop at the tea shop with me," Shu-chang said.

"I've time, no problem." Her grin revealed gaps where her teeth were missing. "There's a nice little shop nearby."

She escorted him past several teahouses to one that was several blocks away. Once they sat down and he saw other customers' food and their tea service, he realized why she'd picked this shop. The tea was among the finest to be purchased in such a town and the dishes were definitely not inexpensive. *Oh well*, he thought, *one good turn deserves another*. He just hoped Uncle Xin, who was really paying for this, would understand.

Once they'd ordered, and after the usual initial pleasantries, Shu-chang said, "Granny, you know more people and get around to more places than almost any other person in town."

She demurred, but was clearly interested in what he was saying. He was aware that he sounded like a pigeon about to be plucked. Granny was a good woman, of that he was sure—after all, Xiang-hua trusted her—but he wondered what she would demand in return for helping them. It could, after all, be dangerous for the elderly woman if the true criminal found out she was gathering evidence against him. Granny might be willing to assist, but at a cost. He coughed and began again.

"What I mean is, with your relationships, you could help me—us—out in finding more about the fire and deaths." He paused, waiting for some sign of agreement.

Granny said nothing; only her slurping tea answered him.

He went on. "I've been able to find out quite a bit about who was around the site and when. But I think I need to expand my questioning."

"Hum," she said, now masticating a stinky tofu.

"One area we have not been able to explore deeply is exactly who the men are who were killed in the fire. We've been working on the premise that they were guards whose bad fate put them at the scene. That their deaths were tragic, but accidental. What if we are wrong? Perhaps the fire was started to hide their murdered bodies."

Granny wiped a hand across her mouth. "I understand, and I'll do what I can. You can count on me."

CHAPTER 19

Xiang-hua stopped in front of the Gao family's entrance and casually examined the polychrome statues standing on either side of the massive doors. Their paint had become worn and chipped with age and weather, but their deeply carved, towering forms were still impressive. She remembered the time she had come here as a child. She had accompanied her grandmother when Mistress Gao had been ill and needed a doctor. Xiang-hua had trembled at the sight of these ferocious door gods and kept close to her grandmother, almost tripping her, as if she could hide under her cloak and be protected.

She shook her head at the memory of her fearful and timid young self. But she'd learned since then how to push away dark thoughts and convince other people—if not herself —of her unquestionable confidence. She discovered that if she acted as if she was in control, clients believed her. Believed *in* her.

Adjusting her medicine bag, she took a deep breath, stepped forward, and rapped loudly on the door.

Once the smaller inner door was opened and the servant saw Xiang-hua standing on the street, his face broke out in a wide grin.

"Mistress is waiting for you," he said, ushering her in. He quickly closed the door and led her to the women's quarters' gate.

Xiang-hua stepped into a small garden surrounded by a veranda dotted with doors leading into the women's private compartments. At the far end a section of the veranda was undergoing repair. Fresh boards and a few tools lay in a nearby pile. One of the women's chambermaids, a middle-aged woman, hurried to the gate and led her past the unfinished woodwork and to Mistress Gao's room.

The heavy fragrance of flowers greeted her even before Mistress Gao herself had a chance to say hello. The luxuriousness of the room—with its porcelain vases, finely painted scrolls hanging from the walls, elaborately carved heavy wood furniture, silk curtains draped around the kang, and silk pillows piled on it—was almost overwhelming. But she had to admit that it was also seductive. While usually quite content with her family's comforts, they could not compare with the fineness and beauty of Mistress Gao's room.

In skirting the pile of tools, the teeth of a saw caught Xiang-hua's hem.

"Oh, I'm so sorry," the maid gushed. Flustered, she blushed, her face growing darker. She rushed to disengage Xiang-hua. Once free, the maid examined the fabric. Dismayed, she looked up at the young doctor. "There's a rip in the material," she said, holding it up.

Xiang-hua took the hem and examined it. "No matter. The rip is small and easily mended."

The maid hesitated and seemed about to say more.

"Your Mistress is waiting for me. This is nothing. Let's go

on." She did not want to cause even more distress for the maid. Xiang-hua had stepped too close to the tools. The unfortunate incident was not the woman's fault.

The maid nodded and they proceeded to the nearest door.

"I'm so glad you came, Sister," Mistress Gao said as they entered. She used an honorific to address Xiang-hua. She patted a place beside her on the kang. "I know the first thing you're going to ask me is how my daughter-in-law is doing. Better. Much better. She's eating and keeping her food down. Of course, she's melancholy, but unfortunately that seems to be her nature."

She glanced up as the two entered the room. Noticing the maid's darkened complexion, she said, addressing the woman: "What's the matter, Lotus? Did something happen?"

The maid's features turned an even darker color. "In passing the worker's tools, a saw caught hold of the Doctor's hem," she said. Her eyes focused on the floor.

"How clumsy of you!" Mistress Gao said to the woman. "To let such a thing happen to our guest." Anger tipped the edges of her words.

Lotus hung her head in silence. She was sure to be punished.

"It was nothing. Nothing. My skirt is fine. It will only take two stiches to mend it," Xiang-hua quickly asserted.

Mistress Gao cast one more glance at the maid, scowled briefly, then turned her attention to Xiang-hua, once more inviting her to join her on the kang.

Xiang-hua settled down amid the luxurious pillows.

"The carpenters working on my veranda haven't been as diligent as they could be. That's the trouble with workers today. Unreliable."

With that, Mistress Gao again addressed her maid. She

waved a hand over a delicate, short bamboo table at her side and the lustrous, blue-on-white porcelain pot and cup sitting on it. "Lotus, take this away and bring us fresh tea and plates of kelp rolls, sausages, and lotus root slices."

Xiang-hua was amused at the mixture of dishes. She hadn't expected a plate of sausages to be included along with the lotus root slices and kelp rolls. Most older women considered sausages to be too *yang*, too strong, for their female constitution and avoided them.

Sitting up, Mistress Gao rested her elbows on the low table. "Now tell me everything you know about the exciting events on the street."

Xiang-hua laughed. "I know very little. Not much has happened since I was here the other day."

"Nonsense. You and Granny are the communication lifeline of every woman in our community. Tell me all the news. The magistrate must have caught the arsonist by now. I'd hate to be that poor boy, what with the accidental deaths of those two men who died in the fire. Have they discovered who they are? Were? Granny said they were San-fu's guards. It's hard to tell because he hires so many vagrants." She paused with a disapproving squint. "I don't know why he does that. They are so unreliable. Always up and leaving without notice. No family. Impossible to find."

Her comments and questions seemed to flow unrestrained. Xiang-hua listened attentively and nodded. She caught the mention of Granny. That meant Mistress Gao was gathering information not only from her but from Granny as well. Were they both inadvertently being sucked into Mistress Gao's information network? To be fair, Xiang-hua thought, wealthy women like Mistress Gao couldn't go out on their own. They remained locked in their luxurious women's quarters and depended on less confined women, like her and Granny, for information on what was happening beyond their own gates. Therefore, a smart, able woman would naturally use as many sources of information available to her as possible.

When Mistress Gao finally took a breath, Xiang-hua said, "I'm sorry to say that the magistrate is still centered on Xiao-ren as the arsonist. He seems to have stopped looking for anyone else."

"Oh, Sister, this is most upsetting for you and your family. But, as I always told your grandmother, that boy was trouble from the start."

Xiang-hua stiffened. This was so unfair. Throwing politeness and caution aside, she found herself saying: "Xiao-ren is not a criminal; he has never been in such trouble before; he's active; he's a boy, that's all." But, even as she said this, images of her father yelling at Xiao-ren for his many transgressions sped across her vision. There were times when he even beat his son, trying to pull him into line. Still, none of that made Xiao-ren an arsonist—or a killer.

Mistress Gao leaned back. "It's hard, I know. I've seen this so many times in so many families. I'm a lot older than you. Believe me, even the best of families have experienced the bad fate of such children." With a softer tone, she said: "I only hope his deeds don't embroil your entire family. I'm confident the courts will show mercy on your father and family since they undoubtedly knew nothing of his terrible deeds."

"Shu-chang will find out who really caused the fire and the deaths," Xiang-hua blurted out. "He's been talking to the merchants and laborers in the area. He's already discovered quite a lot and will prove Xiao-ren's innocence shortly," she lied. She just couldn't let Mistress Gao think Xiao-ren was the criminal.

"He's that new teacher for the Xin clan school, isn't he?"

"Yes. He's new to town, but he's related to the Xins through his mother's side."

"I heard that he's to be honored in a special ceremony by the magistrate himself."

Glad at the change in topics, Xiang-hua said, "He scored number one in the recent provincial examines and he's the first from this district to have done so." She stopped suddenly. She didn't want to insult Master Gao, who had not only passed the second exam, but also the third and final exam—although not as the top candidate.

Mistress Gao cast her eyes to the left, then said, "You don't have to apologize. I understand, that although Master Gao passed at the highest level, he was only among the top half of those who passed. Nevertheless, his achievement has brought great honor to our district and town," she said diplomatically and shifted on her pillows. "Shu-chang seems like a remarkable man. And, he's living in your house?"

Xiang-hua felt her face grow hot. "He lives in a spare room in the compound we share with Uncle Xin." Her family lived in a traditional extended family home. The building was U-shaped. The center rooms comprised her grandparents living area and the main reception room. The side arms had been added for the sons they expected to have to live in once they grew, married, and had families. In the center of the spacious U was a courtyard with a connecting veranda running around it. Today Uncle Xin and his family lived on one side and Xiang-hua's father and his family lived on the other arm of the U. Was she implying that Shu-chang's being in her family home—a home with an unmarried daughter— was not proper?

"Within your compound?"

"Yes, it's connected to the school," Xiang-hua said, pointing out its convenience for his work as teacher.

"You have a room large enough to be a school room, plus another connected to that? How fortunate."

Xiang-hua squirmed. "Those rooms are all on the right arm of our compound. They were originally built to mirror our own family's room on the left of the main building. My grandfather thought he would have many sons and he prepared for them by building a set of legs on each side of his main rooms."

"Yes, I remember your grandmother telling me about that, now that you mention it. But, then, only one son, your father, survived to adulthood. Your Uncle Xin is your father's cousin, through your great-grandfather."

Xiang-hua wanted to change the conversation. It had gotten much too personal. In the Chinese tradition that kinship relationship made Xiang-hua and Shu-chang ideal marriage partners.

Thus, it could be considered improper for them to live together in such close quarters. She quickly changed the subject: "Tell me more about Erh-xi-fu before I go see her."

"Ah, yes," she said, dropping the topic of who lived where and why. "Well, as I said, she's doing better. If she progresses, she should be strong enough to produce a grandson for us." She almost glared at Xiang-hua. "Right? I want that to be your goal as a doctor. She must produce a grandson to keep our family line."

"She seems, as you say, depressed. Can you tell me anything that might help me understand her better? What's she like normally? What was her family like?"

Mistress Gao wrinkled her nose in disgust. "She comes from a good family. Granny brought her to us as a possible second wife for San-fu. As you know, his first wife never produced a child. Totally useless." She pushed the tray away with such force that the tea kettle almost toppled. "San-fu and

Erh-xi-fu's horoscopes matched and she was young enough to produce many children, so we agreed to the second marriage. However, she is difficult and we have had to discipline her."

Xiang-hua sipped her tea and remained silent, listening.

"She must have whined to her family about it," she looked at Xiang-hua as if expecting her to commiserate with her on this. Seeing no reaction, she went on, "After a short time, her brother, of all people, shows up on our door, claiming he's come to 'straighten things out.' Now what do you think that means? His sister is now a part of our family and should abide by our rules. He should not have even been here, but we were polite and let him in the house." She paused, picked up a dried fruit and tore it to bits between her fingers. "He got into a heated argument with my son over his wife's treatment. Can you imagine that?" Her voice rose in indignation.

Xiang-hua grimaced thinking what "treatment" involved with her vulnerable patient.

"Erh-xi-fu hasn't mentioned her brother. Is he still here? How did he and your son settle this, er, problem?"

Mistress Gao slipped another piece of fruit off the plate. "When he first came, he wanted his sister to leave with him. But, of course, that would be impossible. She's married after all; there was nothing he could do."

"Is he still here?" Xiang-hua repeated.

The older woman again shifted positions, picked up the sleeve of her robe, and caressed it. "He returned home."

"When was this?"

"Oh, several days ago. Yes, I remember now, the day before the fire."

"You're certain it was the day before?"

Mistress Gao stiffened, "Of course. Do you think I'm going senile?"

"No, of course not," she said and quickly changed the topic to smooth out the older woman's growing irritation.

With that, Xiang-hua escaped to her patient as soon as possible.

As she came into the room, Xiang-hua was pleased to see Erh-xi-fu not only sitting up, but working on a piece of embroidery.

"I'm doing so much better, Sister. I'm sure I won't need any further treatments," the young wife announced cheerfully.

Xiang-hua shook her head. "I'll decide that." She wasn't ready to leave this defenseless young wife on her own. She was sure that as long as she appeared at the mansion on a regular basis, her mother-in-law's harsh treatment would be lessened. As for the husband's behavior toward his young wife, Xiang-hua couldn't be sure either way. "You feel well today, but without medical care your malaise will return and you'll not have normal menstrual periods. We must stay with the regimen I have set out."

Erh-xi-fu put down her embroidery with a slight pout. "You know best."

As Xiang-hua set out to treat the Erh-xi-fu, she said, "I understand your brother came to see you recently. How nice. Is he still here or has he returned home?"

Erh-xi-fu frowned. "He seems to have left."

"He didn't say goodbye to you before leaving?"

Erh-xi-fu let out a long breadth before answering. "He and my husband had an argument. As I told you, San-fu has been very irritable lately and nothing I did was good enough. He constantly found reason for complaint, as did his mother."

"He beat you," Xiang-hua said, thinking back on their first conversation.

She hung her head and whispered a barely audible: "Yes."

"And his mother."

She slumped even more, didn't look up, and softly answered: "Yes."

"You wrote your parents about how you were treated here, therefore, your brother knew?"

She looked up, her eyes pleading for understanding. "Yes. But I didn't mean for him to come here."

"But you did want to go back home, to leave your marriage?"

"I wanted to go home. I thought if I left San-fu would eventually calm down and call for me to come back."

Xiang-hua didn't bother to ask about what she thought her mother-in-law would do. Some things you just had to accept. We all had our separate fates. Today's life was either a gift for good deeds or retribution for bad deeds from one's past lives. We could ameliorate, but not completely avoid, our fate.

"What happened? Why didn't your brother take you with him?"

"I don't know. In truth, I expected—hoped—I'd be going back to my parents' home with him. I told you they'd had an argument, and I distinctly heard my brother say he was going to take me with him. But the next morning he'd left and never even said good-bye." Tears rolled down her cheeks.

"What did San-fu or Mistress Gao say about that?"

"My mother-in-law said that my brother had agreed I should stay. She'd promised him I'd get treatment so I could get pregnant. So, he returned home to tell my parents." She sighed. "And now, you're here."

Xiang-hua nodded. "So why didn't he tell you or at least say good-bye?"

"My mother-in-law said he was too sad to see me, and asked her to give me his farewells."

Xiang-hua thought about this. That could very well have happened. Failing to save his sister from a difficult marriage could have embarrassed him enough that he chose to simply leave without having to face her with his failure.

Xiang-hua couldn't help but wonder at the timing of his leaving. Was he really content with Mistress Gao's assurances of re-doubling efforts at making sure his sister got pregnant? Did he really believe that would improve her relationship with a brutal husband? The questions filled her mind as she left her patient.

CHAPTER 20

Xiang-hua went straight from the Gao mansion to Granny's house, hoping she'd catch her at home. Of course, she knew the chance of finding Granny there was always slim; she was out most of the day. Her job, after all, was to visit those women who were confined to the house and their family's women's quarters. They all had needs: shopping for common or exotic goods, news about other families, assistance in the younger women's pregnancies and child-births. The other part of her day was spent visiting merchant shops and carts in her pursuit of fulfilling the women's requests.

However, it was early afternoon, a time of rest, so she hoped to find Granny doing just that—or at least home preparing her medicines while the majority of the town rested.

Xiang-hua wandered down a myriad of streets and finally came to an unassuming, diminutive temple of great age at the end of an alley. Sticks of burning incense had recently been placed in a large, carved basin of sand. The sweet fragrance of saffron and other herbs blended with sharp cooking odors from the tightly clustered, open doorways surrounding the temple.

Xiang-hua stepped up to one of the open doors and called into the dim interior: "Granny, it's Xiang-hua."

"Ah, Sister. Have you eaten?" Granny said, using a typical greeting.

"Yes," she lied politely as she stepped into the room.

Granny handed her a three-legged stool. "Let's sit outside." She grabbed another stool, dragging it slightly over the hardened dirt floor to move it. "The air is good for us."

Xiang-hua caught a brief glimpse of Granny's simple one room house. It resembled many homes Xiang-hua visited. The ubiquitous brick kang at the back of the room filled half of the living space and a cooking stove took up one of the remaining corners near the only small window. To her left, several pots sat on the ground near a shelf overflowing with clay containers. A small table crowded with more clay bowls stood on the other side of the door. The only difference in Granny's home from the other such houses was that hers was crammed full with containers of the herbs. Containers she used as a midwife.

The two settled outside Granny's door in a golden shaft of afternoon light.

"Warms the bones," Granny said appreciatively.

They sat amicably together. The heated wall supported their backs and infused them with a welcome warmth.

"I heard Qiu's wife had her baby," Xiang-hua said.

"Yes, a difficult delivery. She always has trouble. But both the baby and Qiu's wife are okay." She frowned. "Next time she and the baby might not be so lucky."

"Doesn't Qiu work for San-fu?" Xiang-hua asked.

Granny squinted up at her. "Did Shu-chang tell you I'd help him gather information where I could?"

"Not exactly, but I thought I, we, could count on you.

Since Xiao-ren is my brother, some people won't tell me anything; others might try to mislead me. The same is true with Shu-chang. Father and Uncle Xin think he can get more people to talk to him, as an esteemed teacher and outsider, but his position also carries some limitations. The very reason one person will tell us everything they know may be the same reason another person won't." She met Granny's eyes. "You're not even considered a part of the equation, so you have access to everyone."

Granny laughed. "All that math is too much for my old ears."

She settled some more into the sun and looked away. "In any case, I did find out something new." She turned back toward Xiang-hua, eyes bright. "It's about San-fu's mother." She paused to check for Xiang-hua's reaction and wasn't disappointed.

"His mother? What could she possibly have to do with this?"

"Well, after Qiu's wife gave birth, I remained in the house watching over her as I usually do. Qiu's mother was there, too. They're from another province and he's her only son. She had to leave her home area to come live with them. A strange town, still, she's quite proud of the living he is able to provide for her and his family."

"Working for the Gao's." Xiang-hua said.

"Hmm-hum. And he likes to tell her stories about his work and the people he works with."

Xiang-hua leaned toward the old woman.

"Apparently, a couple of henchmen working for San-fu do double duty by also working for his mother."

Xiang-hua pursed her lips, thinking of the unfinished veranda repairs in the Gao family's women's quarters. "How did she contact the men when she had jobs for them to carry out? You know men are not allowed in the women's quarters. Wouldn't she have to go through her son?"

Granny held up a palm stopping Xiang-hua's stream of questions. "You're like all the young people these days, too much in a hurry to get to the end before you understand the beginning and middle."

Xiang-hua felt her neck and face get hot. And it didn't come from the sun. She looked down.

"Perhaps the first contact was made through her son, but after that, she would certainly have her own ways of getting in touch with them when she needed to have work done. It's her job to run an efficient and well-maintained house.

"Mistress Gao has always been a strong woman, no doubt. She believes a woman becomes a part of her husband's family, and that's where her place in the world is and should be. When her husband died a few years ago, her father-in-law was still able and a leader in both the community and his family. San-fu did most of the daily business, but his grandfather held the reigns, keeping both his daughter-in-law and his grandson in line."

Xiang-hua nodded. She had heard all of this before. Further, her grandmother often said Mistress Gao's greatest personal sorrow was that she had only produced one living son. She had given birth to other children, but they had all died at birth or soon after. Mistress Gao considered it to be her greatest failure because it meant the Gao family line hung on one person: San-fu.

"I don't understand," Xiang-hua said. "Grandfather Gao is still alive. San-fu has a second wife, who may give him a son. Everything seems to be the same. What has this to do with the warehouse fire?"

Granny shot her a thoughtful look. Xian-hua wanted to say more but remained silent.

"Yes, the grandfather is still alive, but have you seen him?" Granny asked.

"No, however, that is not unusual. I only meet with Mistress Gao because I care for her daughter-in-law. I have no reason to see Grandfather Gao."

"Right. Except that *no one* has seen him for almost a year. According to Qiu's mother, the gossip among San-fu's workers is that he's senile. He's kept away from people so no one knows how disabled he is. All those orders that go out as if they were from him are actually from San-fu who's running everything as he wishes. Even his mother has no control over him."

Xiang-hua nodded. She knew this, but so what?

The sun had moved away and no longer warmed them. Granny pulled her thin jacket closer around her shoulders and continued without pause.

"It's no secret that San-fu has been trying to take control over the Xin lands that had been placed under the protection of his grandfather and give them over to others within the Gao clan. That'd ensure their loyalty as he builds up his power base," Xiang-hua said. She frowned, then released a pent-up breath. This just seemed to be moving in the direction of proving with even more certainty—as if that was needed—the Xin clan members' anger and hatred for San-fu. It wasn't the news she wanted.

"But, besides building a power base, San-fu wants even more wealth. His grandfather's responsibility for collecting the Emperor's taxes, which he now carries out under his grandfather's name, has offered the perfect opportunity. He started increasing the tax burden on the farmers and merchants, not reporting the correct percentage to the government, and keeping the difference. Unfortunately, he chose to keep the excess rice and other goods—the silk, wine, so on—in the same warehouse as the Emperor's," Granny said.

Xiang-hua brightened. "Which was supposed to be inspected by an Imperial Inspector the day of the fire."

"Exactly."

"So, the fire wasn't set for revenge. The best revenge would have been for the Emperor's Inspector to find all of San-fu's illegal goods. Although unlikely, it could have been an accident. Stranger things happen." Xiang-hua breathed a long sigh and gazed up at the ancient temple. A sense of peace she hadn't felt in days started to come over her.

Granny shook her head. "You may be letting your desire to protect your brother cloud your thinking."

At Xiang-hua's bristling, she went on. "Let's think about this. Besides, that's not the story Qiu told his mother." Granny licked her lips. "Wouldn't an accident be pretty convenient? There just happened to be a fire in the very warehouse that held San-fu's ill-gotten goods on the night before the Imperial Inspector was to arrive?"

Xiang-hua threw up her hands. "I know. But, it could have been an accident," she said, desperation pushed her to not give up this alternative solution so easily. She glanced at Granny shaking her head. "All right. I can see you have more to say. What else is there?"

Granny grinned broadly, showing her intermittent teeth. "Mistress Gao often used a couple of her son's most reliable men to do odd jobs around the family's large compound."

Xiang-hua nodded. It made sense, but by itself did not prove anything.

"These men sometimes also put pressure on people who had personal loans with her and were late in their payments." Granny went on: "As I said before, it's easy for her to have contact with them because she manages the mansion."

Xiang-hua smiled, the pieces were beginning to fall into

place. "Under the guise of meeting with her as domestic handymen, these henchmen also acted as her spies. San-fu certainly would not tell her about his illegal activities, but she knew all about his collecting and storing the goods."

"Right," Granny said. "According to Qiu's mother, Mistress Gao was terrified. Defrauding the Emperor of his taxes was the most serious crime one could commit. If anyone found out what her son was doing, it would destroy the Gao family. And not just their family line, but possibly the entire clan.

"She had to stop him. Apparently, she confronted him several days ago about his activities, but he just said not to worry, he knew what he was doing. She threatened to go to his grandfather. He laughed and told her that would be priceless, since the old man didn't even know what day it was.

"Still, the argument put him in a bad mood and he ranted and raved at work. He drank too much and complained to his companions about his interfering mother. Qiu was there and heard the whole thing, as were the two henchmen working for his mother."

"Ah, and those two men reported San-fu's drunken ramblings to his mother," Xiang-hua said.

Granny scrunched her face and slowly wagged her head from side to side. "As you can imagine, she was furious. She and her son argued heatedly and frequently over the next couple of days. Then, when she heard the Imperial Inspector had arrived, she panicked and ordered her henchmen to burn down the building. To throw the court off track, she tried to implicate Xiao-ren.

"She had the warehouse burned to save her family's reputation and to keep her son out of court, where his punishment would most certainly be severe." Granny pursed her lips and nodded sadly as she finished. Xiang-hua sat in a cloud of mixed emotions. She hoped this information would free her brother and save the Xin clan. At the same time, she felt a deep sadness for what this meant not only for the Gao family but for the Gao clan. There were no winners here. She pitied Mistress Gao, who brought this destruction onto the very family she wanted so desperately to save.

CHAPTER 21

Shu-chang strode through the town's streets on his way to the Qiu home. He was energized and excited by Xiang-hua's news from Granny and wanted to speak with Qiu as soon as possible. Granny hadn't been able to tell Xiang-hua who Mistress Gao's henchmen were, just that there were two men who regularly worked for her.

Although Xiang-hua had tried to discover their identities from the Gao servants, they were no help. Shu-chang understood their predicament: much as they liked Xiang-hua, they liked their jobs more. The most she had been able to find out was that they were cousins from another southern province. He hoped Qiu would be more forthcoming.

Xiang-hua had given him directions to the Qiu home, which was on the other side of town, past the warehouse. He didn't give much notice to the remaining gawkers or to the workers as he passed the blackened block. A sharp turn to the left brought him into a small alley lined with old men and women sitting outside doorways. The men played a noisy guessing game as they sat together. Sitting in twos, their fingers flew out at each other while they shouted out a number. Whoever called the correct number of fingers show-ing, won the round. Usually, this was a drinking game; however, since they didn't have alcohol, they improvised. The loser having to stand and bow to the winner with much laughter and badgering by the winner. Then the contestants rapidly played another round. Ignoring the men's noisy display, the women sat quietly on stools with buckets and bowls, cleaning vegetables for dinner.

He stopped at the first group of elders at the mouth of the alley. "Do you know Qiu? He works for San-fu."

The two men nodded in unison. "Fourth door on the right," one fellow said, pointing.

The door was shut tight. Shu-chang hesitated. He'd learned a little about the family: that Qiu's wife just had a baby and wasn't well; that they lived in a modest, one-room house. Therefore, he knew that one room would be where the family worked, ate, and slept. He studied the closed door. Perhaps this wasn't a good idea after all. As he floun-dered, trying to decide what to do, the door opened and a middle-aged woman came out carrying a bucket full of leafy greens.

"Mrs. Qiu?" Shu-chang ventured.

Startled at a stranger asking for her, she moved to step back into the house.

"I am looking for your son." Shu-chang said quickly.

She squinted at him, looking him over, and finally said, "He hasn't returned from work. It's too early."

"Do you know when he will return?

"When he's finished. It's difficult to say when."

Disappointed, he nodded, thanked her, and left, passing the old men once more. They looked up at him.

"Not there?" one asked.

Shu-chang nodded.

"Could've told you that." The other nodded in agreement.

"You the new teacher that the magistrate is fixing to cele-brate?" the first asked.

Shu-chang agreed that he was the teacher. He was impressed with how information got around. He would expect that in a village, but not in a town this size. No notices had been sent out, yet everyone seemed aware of the big upcoming event.

With all this gossip, why is so little known about the fire? he complained silently to himself. To him, that silence in itself was a strong indication the fire really was an accident and not arson. If it was an accident, then the Gaos would be held accountable and be severely punished by the courts for failure of duty. That is, failure to protect the Emperor's taxes. San-fu's family would lose their elite position, which they held through his grandfather, bringing disaster on everyone in the town, in both the Gao and Xin clans. To Shu-chang such an outcome created a critical reason for San-fu to want to make the fire a criminal offense and to push the blame onto someone else. But how could he convince the magistrate? San-fu controlled the burned-out warehouse's site. He allowed access only to his men, on the pretext they were removing debris, which caused a safety hazard. And destroying evidence in the process. Evidence that could prove Xiao-ren innocent.

"You'll find Qiu drinking with San-fu at the Lucky Duck wine shop. It's on the block next to the warehouse, same side of the road," one of the elders volunteered.

Shu-chang thanked them and walked slowly back, lost in thought. Qiu could be in the wine shop a long time and there was no way Shu-chang could talk to him without San-fu knowing.

Mulling over what he could do, he neared the Lucky Duck. A surge of raucous voices enveloped him as he passed the door. He didn't look in. He checked out the opposite side of the street to see if there was a tea house or wine shop he could sit in while keeping an eye on the Lucky Duck. None. All of the shops sold goods of various types, but that's not what he needed. He trudged on, while watching men pushing overloaded wheelbarrows and hauling debris out of the wreckage. Among the laborers, he recognized Zhou and his friends. With a quick glance at the Lucky Duck, Shu-chang hurried toward them.

Zhou saw him coming and stepped off the pile they were dismantling.

"Teacher," he said in greeting.

"Zhou, I need to talk to you."

Zhou tossed a charred block of wood onto a nearby cart and grasped its handles. With a quick nod to the side, he said: "We'll meet you behind the shed."

He hefted the load and dragged the half-empty cart away. Lin and Fang followed, each carrying a large chunk of timber on his shoulder.

Shu-chang quickly moved down the street and around the block. He arrived behind the shed just as the others did.

He explained that he wanted to find out who the two henchmen were who did double duty by working for both San-fu and his mother, Mistress Gao.

Zhou grinned. "Why didn't you say so?" He waved a hand in the direction of a group of men scooping piles of ruined rice onto carts. "That's the Lang cousins, Tou-fu and Mien."

Shu-chang scowled at the names. Was Zhou making fun of him and just making up ridiculous names for the men? "What did you say their names were?" he asked, not trying to hide his skepticism.

Zhou laughed. "Tou-fu and Mien. They both like to eat. A lot. They're big guys. I don't know their real names. It's what everyone around here calls them."

Shu-chang nodded. It made sense. Nick-names were often used instead of given names.

Zhou jerked his head toward a couple of heavyset men working on the rubble. "They're right over there."

"I would like to talk to them. Can you get them for me?"

"No problem."

As Zhou turned to go, Shu-chang added, "Do not tell them I am here. Make something up."

Zhou grinned and nodded.

Shu-chang motioned for Lin and Fang to slide around the shed so the men couldn't see them. Once hidden, they silently waited. It was not long before Zhou rounded the building with the two men in tow.

As soon as the two saw Shu-chang, Lin, and Fang, they balked.

"What's this?" They glared at Zhou. "What're you up to?" Tou-fu started back with Mien following. Zhou stepped in front of them while Lin and Fang flanked their sides, blocking their exit.

"I need to talk to you two," Shu-chang said. "I know what you have done. You might as well confess." He hoped his sounding certain would scare them into telling him more.

Mien sneered at him. "You don't know anything. We didn't do anything."

"I know you work for Mistress Gao."

Tou-fu shot a glance at his cousin. Mien said, "So what? We work for both San-fu and his mother. We need the extra money, that's all."

"And does working for Mistress Gao include doing whatever she orders? Including committing crimes?"

Tou-fu again shot Mien a look. This time Shu-chang thought he recognized fear in the exchange.

"Nonsense. We're simple laborers. We build and repair, that's all," Mien bluffed.

"You build fires for her?" Shu-chang suggested.

Now there was no mistaking the look of fear on Tou-fu's face. "Mistress Gao said she'd protect us, no matter what."

Mien grabbed his cousin's arm. "Stop, idiot. He doesn't know anything." He looked around at Zhou, Lin, and Fang.

"You cannot escape," Shu-chang said. "But if you confess now, the magistrate will be lenient with you. After all, you were only the instruments."

The cousins looked at the four men surrounding them. Zhou and his friends held heavy pieces of wood. Shu-chang stood before them with his hands behind his back, as if he were the judge. The white of his mourning robe added a suggestion of the threat of death for the unrepentant.

"We carried the body to the warehouse, put it on a pile of wood and lit it. Then we lit several fires around the building to make sure everything burned," Tou-fu blurted out.

Shu-chang's mind reeled. *Body? Did he say "body?" What was he talking about?* With concerted effort, he hid his surprise. "The fire was to hide evidence of both the illegal goods and the body?"

"We don't know nothing about illegal goods," Mien said. "Mistress Gao called us in late in the day and said she had a job for us. Turned out she poisoned this guy and had to get rid of his body."

"Did she tell you she'd poisoned him?"

"Not in so many words."

"Then what makes you think so? San-fu could have done him in."

Tou-fu shook his head and Mien said: "The guy was in Mistress Gao's room, half falling out of a chair at her table."

"Nevertheless, how do you know she was the one to poison him and not her son?"

Mien shrugged. "Because she said we had to get him out

quickly. Without her son seeing anything. She didn't want him to find out about the body."

"So, you two decided on your own to put him in the warehouse and burn it down to hide the murder. Why didn't you just dump him along the road somewhere?"

The two shook their heads.

"She told us what to do: take him to the warehouse and set the body and the place on fire. Everything had to be destroyed. No one was to be able to identify the dead man." Mien smirked again. "We did it, too. Nobody ever guessed who the guy was. Thought he was one of San-fu's guards. Could've been, but wasn't." He grimaced and looked down at the ground. "One of his guards was asleep and we didn't know he was in the warehouse. Too bad. He burned to death. His bad fate."

Shu-chang didn't fail to notice that Mien didn't take any responsibility for his actions. Everything was someone or something else's fault. He was disgusted with their lack of morality and had to struggle to keep a passive demeanor.

"But you don't know who the dead man was? You hadn't seen him before?" Shu-chang asked.

"We didn't know and didn't need to know," Mien said.

Shu-chang stroked his chin. This was so much worse than he'd thought.

"Zhou, Lin, and Fang, tie their hands with their belts. Escort these men to the court with me."

CHAPTER 22

If they had been at the yamen in the district capital, Shu-chang would have struck an enormous gong in the administration's courtyard, alerting the court that he had a complaint. Since this was the Gao mansion's courtyard, there was no official gong. He worried that if the servant they had to go through to carry the message to the magistrate was one of Gao's that they would be turned away.

Upon arrival, however, Shu-chang was pleased to find that they were led directly into a private courtyard, which had been temporarily set up for the magistrate's needs. Shu-chang relayed his grievance through one of the magistrate's own assistants. Fortunately, earlier the Xin family had generously gifted this assistant in the family's attempts to grease the wheels of justice. He recognized Shu-chang and immediately brought his case before the judge.

In short order, Shu-chang was allowed to go before the court. With his entourage following, he entered the Gao family's impressive reception room, which was lined along two sides with parallel rows of dark, wooden chairs. Grand scrolls of calligraphy and delicate paintings hung on the walls.

Amongst this finery, guards holding weapons stood at attention. At the end of the large hall, the magistrate sat behind an immense, ornately carved, black-lacquered table. This was the magistrate's make-shift courtroom.

Leaving his men and the prisoners, Shu-chang strode forward. Halting in front of the judge, he bowed. The magistrate watched him with an alert, though quizzical, expression. Shu-chang hoped that since the judge had told him to keep the court appraised of anything he discovered about the fire, that his bringing in these men and not simply reporting them to the court would be acceptable. He did not want to be accused of interfering with the court business. On the other hand, he was not only about to accuse two drifters without ties to the community but also two members of the most powerful family in the district. If the magistrate believed he was bringing false charges against the Gao family, his career was over before it had begun.

Shu-chang steadied his breathing and tried to still his heart.

"What is your reason for coming before the court?" the judge asked, peering over at him.

Shu-chang covered one hand over the other and raising them in front of his chest he bowed before the judge. There was no turning back now. "Your Honor, I have brought the men who started the warehouse fire, Lang Tou-fu and Lang Mien."

The judge looked up at the two men Shu-chang had brought in with him, their hands tied behind their backs; heads down.

"State your complaint against these two," the judge said.

"They have confessed to the crimes of starting the warehouse fire. Three other men heard this confession. They burned the building on the orders given by one of their employers. Mistress Gao."

At that, the magistrate struck his table. "Are you accusing Mistress Gao of the crime?"

"Your Honor, as you will hear when you interrogate them, Mistress Gao hired them to destroy the building and its contents," Shu-chang said, determined to keep his resolve.

"This is a very serious accusation. Be careful what you say. What reason could she have for such a thing?" the magistrate queried. The threat in his words unmistakable.

"From what I determined through my investigations, Mistress Gao had two reasons for such an action." Shu-chang took a deep breath and proceeded to reiterate all that Granny and Xiang-hua had learned about San-fu's abuse of the tax system and his storing of his illegal gains in the government warehouse; about his mother's concern that when the court found out about his illegal activity, he and the whole family would be punished, bringing an end to their family line. Something she would never allow to happen.

When Shu-chang finished with this long, sorry tale, the magistrate rapped his fingers on a pile of papers before him. "That is reason enough for the fire. And I will certainly investigate your charge thoroughly." He frowned at Shu-chang. "You had better be right. To bring a false accusation against an innocent person is a serious crime in itself."

Shu-chang nodded. "This is the truth as far as I know it," he said.

The magistrate studied the young scholar. "But, you also said there was a second reason. What is that?"

"The second concerns hiding a murder."

The magistrate's eyes opened wide and he glared at the men beside Shu-chang.

"These men are not the murderers, Your Honor, although they are the ones who disposed of the body." Then Shu-chang proceeded to tell him about what Xiang-hua had learned from Erh-xi-fu. "Earlier in the day before the fire, the entire household heard Erh-xi-fu's brother having a fierce argument with San-fu in which he apparently said he was going to take his sister back home because of the brutal treatment she'd been receiving in the Gao household. San-fu said that would be impossible; she was his wife and would remain in the mansion.

"After San-fu went to work, Mistress Gao invited Erh-xi-fu's brother into her chamber to talk with him. Before going to see her, he told his sister that he expected Mistress Gao wanted to smooth things out. He hoped she'd let Erh-xi-fu leave with him. That was the last time Erh-xi-fu saw her brother. Her mother-in-law sent a maid over with the message that her brother had returned home after agreeing that his sister would remain in the household and that she would be taken care of.

"Apparently, however, such was not the case. Later Mistress Gao called Lang Tou-fu and Lang Mien to her rooms. There they found a man slumped over her table, dead. They thought she'd poisoned him. She told them she wanted to get the body out of the house before her son saw it. From this I deduce two things: The body was Erh-xi-fu's brother and San-fu knew nothing of the murder. If he had, his mother wouldn't worry about hiding the body from him."

The magistrate stroked his beard and nodded.

"And you contend it was Mistress Gao who specifically ordered the Lang cousins to take the body to the warehouse. Therefore, the fire in the warehouse—which she wanted to look like arson—was to hide Mistress Gao's own crime of murder and her son's crime of stealing from the Emperor," the magistrate said.

"Yes, Your Honor."

The magistrate angrily glanced around him. Shu-chang noted that his gaze settled on an ancient scroll with a well-known saying written in bold characters:

Be content with what you have

The magistrate shook his head. "If what you say is true, the malicious and irresponsible behavior of these two will bring down the entire family."

After interrogating Lang Tou-fu and Lang Mien, the judge brought in various Gao servants, who, one by one, corroborated what Shu-chang had reported. After deciding not to interview Erh-xi-fu due to her illness and because there was no evidence that she had been involved or known about any of the crimes, he brought in Mistress Gao and San-fu.

Shu-chang, Uncle Xin, and Chu stood off to one side at the back of the room, listening.

Shu-chang could see Mistress Gao's defiance as her maid led her through the curious crowd and into the room. She was livid at being brought in as a commoner before the court. After all, her father-in-law was a *jin-shi*, a high-status degree holder. However, as soon as she saw the judge, she controlled her anger and put on her most pleasing face. She bowed low before the bench.

"Mistress Gao, you know the accusations against you: murder of your daughter-in-law's brother, organizing the burning of a government warehouse and destruction of its goods, and misleading the court. If you tell me everything, the court will be lenient in your punishment."

"This is all a terrible situation caused by dishonest members of the Xin clan, who are trying to annihilate the Gao clan."

The judge frowned. "I warn you. You must not try to mislead the court."

She trembled in her fury. "I am not the one to mislead the court. That is the one," she pointed to Shu-chang. "He has spun a tangle of lies about me and my son in order to save his mother's cousins."

"Madam, the court has interviewed many witnesses who corroborate the details of your crimes." He glared over the table at her. "Even though the law forbids the use of severe torture to elicit the truth from the elderly and from women, I still have means at my disposal. Do you understand?"

Shu-chang was taken aback by the magistrate's threat. Would he actually beat her or use the finger squeezer on her? While not as painful and torturous as some devices, it could crush the victim's finger, causing permanent injuries.

The judge's words had an immediate impact on Mistress Gao. "I understand." She seemed to sag against her maid. But she quickly rallied and declared in a clear, righteous voice, "It is the duty of a daughter-in-law to maintain the family, both by producing descendants and by protecting the family line. San-fu had created a serious problem for us by being overly zealous in collecting taxes. And perhaps in keeping a larger percentage than he should have. I needed to correct that and quickly. The only way was to destroy the excess goods."

"By burning the government warehouse," the judge said.

She paused, then nodded. She couldn't help but add, however: "How he could have been so careless as to keep the goods in the same building as the tax revenue is beyond me." As if considering this transgression, she pouted with irritation.

"And your daughter-in-law's brother?"

She looked up at this, her eyes wide and innocent. "Well, he wanted to take his sister, San-fu's *wife*, away. That would never do. She was young and could produce many children."

"He wanted to take her because she was ill-treated in your house," the judge pointed out.

She shrugged. "She has to toughen up. What daughter-in-law doesn't complain about their mother-in-law and even her husband?"

Shu-chang thought of the bruises Xiang-hua told him she'd seen on Erh-xi-fu and on the girl's desperate attempt at suicide to escape their abuse.

"It was easy. If he weren't there, she wouldn't leave. He had to go."

"You mean die," the judge said.

"Well, yes. I invited him in for tea and poisoned him." She seemed to perk up. "The problem was how to get rid of his body. Killing him was easy, but not getting rid of his body. Where was I to put it so that he wouldn't be found and recognized?

"That's when I thought of having Tou-fu and Mien take him over to the warehouse. The timing worked out so well, really. It was as if the gods themselves wished for our success." She nodded to herself, but then, her lips twisted in annoyance once more. "It almost worked, too, except for him and that meddling Xiang-hua." She stared angrily at Shu-chang standing among the crowd of on-lookers lined up against a side wall.

The magistrate had her removed from the room before calling her son to be interrogated.

San-fu had none of his mother's bravado. He stumbled into the room between two powerful guards. At the sight of the magistrate, he dropped to his knees and kowtowed before the judge.

"San-fu, you are the collector of revenue for the district and are charged with stealing tax revenue from the Emperor and misleading the court in its investigation. What have you to say?" the magistrate's voice rang out.

"Your Honor, as collector of revenue for His Highness, I have mistakenly miscalculated the taxes owed and collected. For that I duly apologize."

The magistrate glowered at him. "Miscalculated? You miscalculated the taxes on the high side only for members of the Xin clan. How do you suppose that happened? And," he went on, "my accountant had recently reported to me that, in reviewing your tax collection records, he noted a distinct disparity between what you collected and what you intended to pass on to the central government. Is that also a 'miscalculation'?"

San-fu hung his head and remained silent.

"We know from your mother that you've stored your ill-gotten goods in the government warehouse, so you might as well admit to stealing from the Emperor."

It didn't take long for San-fu to break down and admit to collecting excess taxes and skimming off the excess for himself. After further extensive questioning, however, it was clear that he had no idea about his mother's murder of his brother-in-law or her plans to burn the warehouse.

Shu-chang was impressed with how this man's bravado turned out to be a paper tiger. It was a lesson he stuck away in the back of his mind: A persecutor, once his web of falsehoods and intimidating behaviors were brought to light, crumbled like a dried leaf.

CHAPTER 23

B ack at Uncle Xin's house, Uncle Xin, Shu-chang, Chu, and Xiang-hua sat drinking tea and eating pumpkin seeds. Shu-chang had just finished telling Xiang-hua what happened at court that day. He noticed tears lining her eyelashes and immediately thought she must be thinking about Xiao-ren.

"Don't worry, Xiang-hua. Xiao-ren is to be released right away. He'll be home soon," he rushed to reassure her.

She wiped a finger against her eyes. "It's not that. I mean, I am concerned about him and I'm so glad he'll be home soon. But I guess I'm just so happy for the whole Xin clan."

Her father and uncle nodded.

"Yes, our small clan has been spared," Uncle Xin said, avoiding looking at Chu.

"What do you think will happen to the Gao family and clan?" Xiang-hua asked.

"From what I understand, Grandfather Gao is too senile and too old to be considered responsible under the law for the actions of any of his family. So, given his reduced mental capacity and age, he won't be charged with anything, nor will he be punished," Shu-chang said.

"Mistress Gao has been charged and found guilty of murder and inciting arson on a government warehouse. She's not old enough to fall under the leniency clause in the law for the elderly, so she will be held responsible to the maximum extent," Uncle Xin added. "And, because she refused to cooperate until forced to do so, she will not necessarily merit any leniency in her punishment for her crimes. After the upper courts have reviewed her case, she will almost certainly get the death penalty, probably through strangulation."

Xiang-hua shuddered. She thought of the many happy hours she had spent in the Gao mansion under her grandmother's tutelage. "Mistress Gao had become obsessed with the continuation of the Gao family line. Probably out of an extreme sense of guilt. She always defined a successful daughter-in-law as one who produced offspring, securing the continuation of the family. She was in danger of failing completely at that. Only one of her children, San-fu, lived to adulthood, and he hadn't, yet, produced any offspring."

Shu-chang nodded. "Not only that, but if the government found out he was stealing tax revenues, he'd be executed. Again, an end to their paternal line. Once she heard that the Imperial Inspector was in town and about to do a review of the collected rice and other tax goods, she panicked and rushed to protect the Gao family line."

They all sat contemplating the irony of her rash actions. No one gloated. Not having progeny was the greatest loss any family could have. Descendants not only took care of the living, they took care of the ancestors as well. Ancestors who had no one to care for them on this side of the living world became dangerous, hungry ghosts, roaming around causing trouble for everyone.

"And what about San-fu?" Xiang-hua asked.

"Because his grandfather has been senile for some time and his father is dead, San-fu is the head of the family. Therefore, he is responsible for his mother's crimes and will also be held accountable."

Uncle Xin nodded. "His punishment will be one degree higher than his mother's. She was his mother, but as a woman, she was under his leadership and care. He should have known what she was doing and prevented it. He didn't fulfill his duties and will be held accountable under the law. He may very well be beheaded."

Voices from outside the door alerted them to Xiao-ren's arrival. He was brought in on a stretcher, surrounded by concerned, but relieved, fellow Xin clan members.

Xiang-hua gasped at the sight of her brother's blood-encrusted clothing, dirty face, and matted hair. His father and uncle immediately started giving orders to the two men carrying him on where to put Xiao-ren down. They also quickly enlisted the other clan members accompanying the stretcher to bring clean cloths, hot bath water, hot tea....

Shu-chang stepped out of the way as the room erupted into controlled chaos. Xiang-hua slipped out of the room and returned presently with her medicine bag. Once her brother was ensconced on the kang, the others stepped back too, allowing Xiang-hua to clean him up and minister to his tortured, bruised, and bloody body.

Shu-chang cringed as he watched her work. If they hadn't solved the case when they did, could his young cousin have held out against the pain any longer? By law, the court couldn't punish a criminal for a serious offense until they'd confessed. Knowing that, many of the guilty simply would not confess. As a result, the government implemented a policy of torturing those arrested. The goal was to bring about the guilty person's acceptance of his responsibility for his crimes.

Shu-chang looked down at the face of the young man—a boy, really. Xiao-ren hadn't confessed. That meant more torture was sure to come, if he'd remained in jail.

Uncle Xin spoke low, comforting words to Chu. Several other men had taken up stools and were discussing the court case. Many cast friendly, appreciative glances at Shu-chang. A few came up, thanked him, and asked about his investigation. He glanced at Xiang-hua as she worked diligently on her brother. They had done this together, with Granny too, of course. He almost smiled. What an odd trio.

One of his students sidled up to him. "Honorable Teacher," he said. "Did you hear what happened to San-fu's wives and his grandfather?"

Shu-chang shook his head. Another of the men in the mix spoke up, "Erh-xi-fu is going back to her family. Word has already been sent to them. Someone will come for her."

"What about Grandfather Gao and the first wife?" Shu-chang asked.

"Since Grandfather Gao has been found to be of insufficient mental capacity, his nephew—his deceased younger brother's son—will now be in charge of clan affairs. The magistrate is allowing old man Gao to live out his life in the family mansion and be cared for by San-fu's first wife, who—in spite of her difficult life in the mansion—has a strong sense of filial piety. She will remain."

"I wonder what will happen to all of the Xin lands," one gruff voice called out.

Several others nodded in concern.

Uncle Xin said, "I've already talked briefly with old man Gao's nephew. Our land fees will return to their original rates and we'll be able to go back to cultivating our own fields once more. It turns out the men San-fu gave the land to were not farmers. The crops suffered even more under them. The Gao clan prefers to have good, hardworking farmers on the land." He grinned sardonically.

"He means better crops even in the worst of times, so more revenue for them," another man shouted. A relieved, nervous laughter filtered through the room.

Xiang-hua admonished them against their noisiness and shooed them out of the room so Xiao-ren could rest. The men slunk out the door, but as they reached the streets their cheerful voices picked up again.

Reflecting on the past couple of weeks, Shu-chang was content with the results for his mother's maternal clan. He was sure the farmers in his home village would also have their land fees returned to normal under the new Gao administrator of the lands. He comforted himself by the realization that by finding the real culprits in Xiao-ren's case, he had helped his own village as well. But—he laid his hand over his eyes—he still hadn't found his father's and uncle's murderers.

———

Being young and resilient, Xiao-ren made a fast recovery. Nevertheless, Xiang-hua kept him at home and wouldn't let him out, not even for school, until she was completely satisfied he had fully recovered. Unfortunately, even with her constant care, the severity of the torture left him with a slight limp on his left side.

Within a few short days, Shu-chang decided it was time for his young cousin to begin his studies once more, so he stopped in to give him some reading material. When he entered the room, Xiang-hua stood at a table blending a medicinal concoction for her brother. She quietly nodded welcome at him and continued her work.

Xiao-ren looked up from a dice game he was playing with another of his friends and greeted him cheerfully. Shu-chang was not happy with his gambling, but forbore making any comments.

"Teacher, I've made a momentous decision and it concerns both of us," Xiao-ren said enthusiastically.

Shu-chang threw a quizzical glance at Xiang-hua. She raised her shoulders in an "I have no idea" response. He looked back at Xiao-ren.

"My life has been spared because of you."

"And because of your sister," Shu-chang corrected.

Xiao-ren ignored him and began again. "My life has been spared because of you. Our karma is intertwined. It's my fate to follow you for the gift of life you've given me. Therefore, I pledge to be your faithful servant from this day forward—for the rest of my life," he added in case Shu-chang misunderstood.

Shu-chang smiled. "That's a long time, Xiao-ren. You may want to rethink this."

The young man adamantly shook his head. "I've made up my mind. It's my fate to be your loyal servant."

Shu-chang raised his eyebrows in surprise at Xiang-hua.

"It's his life," she said shaking her head and grinning broadly.

Shu-chang stared back at the robust youth, unsure of whether this outpouring of loyalty was a gift or a curse.

At last, assured that Xiao-ren would recover, Shu-chang returned to his room. Lying on his bed, he reflected over the past few days. He was pleased at being a part of not only bringing Xiao-ren to safety, but also removing suspicion from other Xin clan members who had suffered so much at the hands of San-fu.

At the same time, he couldn't shake a sense of malaise.

Shu-chang turned over and over. One thought dominated his thoughts, overshadowing his successes: He had done nothing to find the murderers of his father and uncle.

San-fu had caused his father and uncle misery by demanding a significantly higher fee for working the land— and had ultimately thrown Shu-chang off of it, which ended with him up here in his mother's brother's village as an itinerant scholar. So, Shu-chang felt a measure of satisfaction that now Gao's grandson would be held accountable for his misdeeds. Nevertheless, at least from what Shu-chang could determine, the bully was not a murderer. At the moment, it looked like he may not be the person behind his father's and uncle's deaths.

Shu-chang turned again on his narrow, wood platform. Its familiar hardness now proved to be more enemy than friend. Sleep eluded him.

Late into the night, he finally fell into a troubling dream state. His father and uncle came to him, disheveled, their bodies bloodied. They pleaded for him to find the men who murdered them, to give them justice. Shu-chang awoke in a sweat. There was more for him to do.

THE END

CHARACTERS WITH
PRONUNCIATION &
DESCRIPTION

Emperor Hongwu
  Hongwu = Hong-woo
  Founding emperor of the Ming Dynasty (1364 – 1644);
ethnic Han Chinese.

Xin Clan
  Xin = Shin
  Includes all people related by blood through the paternal,
Xin, side of the family; all have Xin surname; minority clan in
town of Jian.

Gao Clan
  Gao = Gaow
  Includes all people related by blood through their paternal, Gao, side of the family; all have Gao surname; largest and
dominant clan in town of Jian.

Characters:
  Hong Shu-chang
  Hong Shu-chang = Hong Shoe-chang

Itinerant scholar. Related to Xin clan through his mother.

Jin-fang

Shu-chang's friend from his home village.

Uncle Xin

Shu-chang's mother's brother.

Aunt Nu-er

Shu-chang's aunt, married to Uncle Xin

Master Gao

Elite elder, once powerful leader in district. Passed the third highest national examination giving him special legal privileges.

Gao San-fu

Master Gao's grandson.

Gao Tan

Member of Gao clan who took over Shu-chang's family land.

Xin Xiang-hua

Xiang-hua = Sheeang-whoa

Second cousin to Shu-chang on his mother's side of the family. Sometimes called by the honorific "Sister."

Xin Xiao-ren

Xiao-ren = Sheeao-wren

Xiang-hua's younger brother, cousin to Shu-chang on his mother's side.

Xin Chu

Uncle Xin's cousin on his paternal side; father to Xiang-hua and Xiao-ren.

Erh-xi-fu

Erh-xi-fu = Er-shee-fu

Gao San-fu's second wife.

Grandmother Yi-po

Yi-po = Ee-poe

Xiang-hua's paternal grandmother. A medical doctor specializing in working with women patients.

Mistress Gao

Matriarch in Gao household; Master Gao's daughter-in-law; San-fu's mother.

Granny

An older woman; midwife; assistant for upper class women confined to their family's homes.

Xin Zhang-lung

Zhang-lung = Jang-lung

Young student in Xin Clan school; brother to Zhang-zong.

Xin Zhang-zong

Zhang-zong = Jang-tzong

Young student in Xin clan school; brother to Xin Zhang-lung.

Lotus

Maid.

Zhou

Zhou = Jo

Migrant laborer from Fuzhou City, Fujian Province.

Lin

Lin = Lynn

Migrant laborer from Fuzhou City, Fujian Province.

Fang

Migrant laborer from Fuzhou City, Fujian Province.

Ba-ren

Man with access to court documents.

Xin Huei

Huei = Whowhey

Hates San-fu because of San-fu's exorbitant land-use fees.

Xin Kan

Xin Huei's father.

Xin Guei-hu

Guei-hu = Guay-hu

Runner for the court.

Chen

Works for Master Gao's family.

Qiu

Qiu = Cheeou

Works for San-fu

Lang Tou-fu

Tou-fu = Toe-fu

Laborer; works for San-fu and his mother. Tou-fu means bean curd.

Lang Mien

Laborer; works for San-fu and his mother. Mien means noodle.

NOTES

Chinese Names

Chinese place the surname, the family name, first and the given name second. For example, in Hong Shu-chang's name, Hong is his surname. Shu-chang is his given name. The surname is passed down through the paternal line.

When a woman marries, she keeps her own family of origin's paternal surname. In some case, she may also be referred to by both her husband's name and her paternal surname—Mrs. Gao nee Ling, for example. However, in this story, I refer to San-fu's mother as simply Madam Gao, using her husband's surname in order to clarify the relationship for the American reader.

Given names: Some families give the sons, or the male cousins, of the same generation two given names. The first is the same for every male child; the second is unique. For example, in **Deadly Relations** there are two brothers whose names are Xin Zhang-lung and Xin Zhang-zong. Xin is their family name; Zhang is the name given to all sons in the family of their generation; and lung and zong are their unique given names.

Clans

Chinese clans are made up of people who are related paternally, that is, through the male line going back to one ancestor. In the town of Jian, there are two clans: the Gao clan, the majority, dominate clan and the Xin, a smaller clan. In southern China, villages and towns were often made up of one or two clans with a scattering of outsiders. Jian is a market town, not a city, therefore it would fit this expectation. Often clans set up private schools for the boys in their clan. This was to help families who could not afford tutors for their boys and to ensure literacy among their members. And, of course, the hope was always that at least one boy in each generation would be bright and diligent enough to pass the all-important government exams.

The Examination System

For hundreds of years China's government has been an amalgam of an Imperial elite determined by blood line and a bureaucracy determined by merit. The Imperial elite ruled the country through its emperor; the vast bureaucracy ran the complex economic, social, judicial, and political everyday life of the nation. The officials holding posts from the provincial through the national level were called scholar-officials because they achieved the right to be considered for a government post through a three-tiered examination system.

At least as far back as the Sui dynasty (sixth century CE) the civil service examination system has served as the gateway to becoming a part of Imperial China's official governing elite. Once a candidate passed the three exams at the very highest levels they were immediately placed in highly responsible government positions which often required technical knowledge. However, the examinations themselves were largely based on the Confucian classics and commentaries on the classics. Boys from a young age spent their lives studying in order to pass the exams and hold a prestigious government office. Very few boys—the brightest, showing great intellectual promise, and usually from wealthier families—took even the preliminary examination at the county level. Schooling for most boys who attended any type of school often ended after five or six years. Thus, giving them enough ability to read and write for everyday needs, that's all. Generally speaking, the literacy rate among boys later in the Imperial Period has been calculated to be about 40 percent. For girls, the rate was considerably lower, probably about 10 percent. Education was expensive and not considered a necessity.

Interestingly, in the early Ming dynasty, there was a military component to the examination system, as well. For example, candidates needed to know how to ride a horse and shoot a bow. This was because, after a bloody civil war in which the nation was wrestled from the hands of the Yuan dynasty's Mongol rulers, the first Ming emperor, Hongwu, wanted his bureaucratic officials to be able to defend the nation against foreign invaders, if necessary.

After passing the county preliminary examination, the candidates were considered students who could go on to take the three major examinations: the first at the prefectural (district) level; the second at the provincial level; and the third at the national level. The latter was given at the imperial palace itself, a highly symbolic location, for it reified the relationship between the the successful candidates and their duty to the emperor and his dynasty.

This examination system created a track for social mobility in imperial China for even the poorest boy and his family—provided he had the inherent ability and economic support needed to study for years in preparation for these gatekeepers. However, the years spent studying were well worth it, for those who passed were immediately placed in a privileged social and legal category, which was advantageous to them and their family. For example, the scholar-officials were 1) relieved of their obligation to pay taxes, and 2) could not be brought into court for a crime they committed until after their certificates were revoked. This was because as scholar-officials they represented the emperor and the emperor could not be hauled before a court or accused of a crime. The practical implication of this was that the merits of a case had to be very solid before any action could/would be taken against a scholar-official.

GLOSSARY

Terms with Pronunciation and Definition

fuchin
    fu-chin
    father

gan-bei
    gan-bay
    Drinking term meaning "drink up!"

guanxi
    guan-shee
    Cultivation of a personal network through such things as gift-giving and exchange of favors.

jie-yuan
    jieh-youan
    The scholar ranked first in the provincial examination, the second level of national examinations. The successful

candidates were eligible to take the third level exams and become scholars at the *jin-shi* level.

jin-shi

gin-shir

The scholar who passed at the nation's highest, third, examination. Only 1-5% of the examinees passed. The successful candidates received many privileges, including special protections under the law.

juren

zhu-wren

A scholar who passed the country's second level examination, that is, the provincial level examination.

kang

kang

A brick platform built at one side of the room; used for sleeping and/or general daily activities.

yamen

yeahmen

Headquarters of the Chinese government and the official residence of the magistrate.

ABOUT THE AUTHOR

P.A. De Voe is an anthropologist with a PhD in Asian studies. Her specialty is traditional China. She has authored several early Ming Dynasty stories, including **The Mei-hua Trilogy** and short stories from Judge Lu's Case Files. Her work has been honored with an Agatha nomination and a Silver Falchion Award. A Judge Lu short story appeared in an Anthony Award winning anthology, **Murder Under the Oaks**, edited by Art Taylor.

www.padevoe.com

OTHER MING DYNASTY MYSTERIES & ADVENTURES BY P.A. DE VOE

Hidden,
A Mei-hua Adventure
Warned,
A Mei-hua Adventure
Trapped,
A Mei-hua Adventure

The Mei-hua Trilogy, a box set (e-book)

Lotus Shoes,
a Mei-hua short story

Judge Lu short stories,
From Judge Lu's Ming Dynasty Case Files

To discover more stories
about Imperial China, visit **padevoe.com**